Taking Off the Tinsel

Edited by
Betty Gibbs,
Chris Levan,
& Wynne Edwards

Rowan Books

Canadian Cataloguing in Publication Data
Main entry under title:
Taking off the tinsel
ISBN: 1-895836-19-0
1. Christmas—Literary Collections.
I. Gibbs, Betty, 1946- II. Levan, Christopher, 1953-
III. Edwards, Wynne Margaret, 1943-
PN6071.C6T34 1996   808.8'033   C96-910542-8

Book design by

Printed and bound in Canada by Priority Printing
Cover photograph taken by Frank Fearn several weeks after the birth and death of Jean and Frank's daughter. It took Jean years to say: "I had two children, but only one is living." Courtesy of Gordon Fearn, who himself took years to untangle Christmas 1949—the year he received his first two-wheeled bicycle, toys enough for two and, strangely, a doll house.

Rowan Books gratefully acknowledges the financial assistance of the Canada Council and the Alberta Foundation for the Arts, a beneficiary of the Lottery fund of the Government of Alberta. Rowan Books is an imprint of
    The Books Collective
    214-21 10405 Jasper Ave.
    Edmonton, Alberta, Canada T5J 3S2
    (403) 448-0590

Acknowledgements

All the works in this anthology have been printed by permission of the authors. Previous publications of any of the works included are noted below:

"A Kind of Christmas Poem" by John B. Lee was originally published in *When Shaving Seems Like Suicide*, Goose Lane Editions, 1992.

"Phone Calls" by Alice Major is from her poetry collection *Time Travels Light*, Rowan Books, 1992.

An earlier version of "Nellie's Vigil" by Gary Langguth appeared in his creative writing thesis *King Street and Other Stories*.

"Christmas On the Other Hand" by Sybil Shaw-Hamm appeared in the *Steinbach Carillon* weekly newspaper, Steinbach Manitoba, Christmas 1993.

"Molly Goes Christmas Shopping" by Anne Swannell was included in her poetry collection *Mall*, published by Rowan Books, 1993.

"Sarasota" by Richard Cumyn appeared in *Acta Victoriana*, The Literary Journal of Victoria University, Volume 118, Number 1.

"Living Colour" by Adele Megann was part of her winning submission for the Bronwen Wallace Memorial Award.

"The Stepfather's Story" by Shirley A. Serviss is from her poetry collection *Model Families*, Rowan Books, 1992.

"The Midwife's Tale" by Mary Woodbury was first published as a play for voices in her collection by the same name, published by Woodlake Books in 1990.

"Crèche" by Bert Almon appeared in his poetry collection *Earth Prime*, Brick Books, 1994.

"The First Blended Family" by Chris Levan first appeared as a column in *The Edmonton Journal*, December 14, 1994.

Contents

Introduction .... *Betty Gibbs* 7

Twas the Night .... *Cliff Burns* 11

Advent .... *Barb Howard* 12

Phone Calls .... *Alice Major* 18

Nellie's Vigil .... *Gary J. Langguth* 20

A Kind of
Christmas Poem .... *John B. Lee* 29

Christmas On the
Other Hand .... *Sybil Shaw-Hamm* 31

Mother & Child .... *Diane Linden* 38

The American
Hotel .... *Wynne Edwards* 39

White .... *Jacqueline Bell* 44

Christmas in
the Country .... *Syr Ruus* 46

The Ice Breakers .... *Anne Swannell* 52

Sarasota .... *Richard Cumyn* 55

Molly Goes
Christmas Shopping .... *Anne Swannell* 67

Playing
Marley's Ghost .... *Timothy J. Anderson* 69

Traverse Afar..................*Alice Major*..................74

The Second
Coming of Internet..................*Dianne Linden*..................75

The Ram..................*Jannie Edwards*..................79

Christmas Eve in
Thumbprint..................*Marie Anne McLean*..................80

Christmas at the
Bissell Centre..................*Gale Sidonie Sobat*..................85

Living Colour..................*Adele Megann*..................89

The
Stepfather's Story..................*Shirley A. Serviss*..................94

The Midwife's Tale..................*Mary Woodbury*..................97

Crèche..................*Bert Almon*..................106

The First
Blended Family..................*Chris Levan*..................107

Contributor
Biographies..................110

Introduction

Betty Gibbs

"All I want for Christmas is..." something beautiful? laughter? that perfect year, the year I was six and got the skates, to happen again and again? or do I just want a faithful spouse? a missing child to come home?

Christmas can give us gifts of happiness, beauty, hilarity, excitement and peace. However, disappointment and disillusion also accompany Christmas more regularly than cranberries do turkey. For the same reason that turkey without cranberries seems unthinkable to some of us, Christmas without happiness, without a "proper" family, without gifts, without food, without music and sparkle and dressing up and parties, seems a contradiction in terms. It's because, whatever our actual experience, we expect these things to happen at Christmas. They are part of our definition of the word.

Our experience tells us that expectation leads to disappointment as often as satisfaction. In fact, the more specific the expectation, the greater the likelihood of disappointment. Everyone knows the problem of shopping when you know precisely what you want. Often there isn't one to be found anywhere. If you can't let go of wanting that specific thing, you are doomed to disappointment. However, if you are still capable of seeing new possibilities and feeling delight in surprise, you can be pleased by what you get instead—the unexpected.

The people of Israel were waiting for a Messiah—they expected a king, but got a baby in a stable. Some made the shift to accept the unexpected and they rejoiced. Whether we were specifically taught this story, whether we believe it or approve of it, it can be found at the heart of both the expectations and disappointments of the Christmas season. It permeates our culture and cannot be ignored.

There's the story of the seemingly perfect family—Mom, Dad and baby. Mom and Dad stick with each other through thick and thin, whatever their worries may be. The story of joy at the birth of the child tells us that children are to be valued and respected because they are the hope of the future. Beauty and magic amidst humble surroundings—angels singing, stars shining, animals talking at midnight, gifts and special visitors—have taught us to expect mystery, glory and love. There is no place in this scene for bitterness, loss, poverty or rage, yet these are equally real in people's lives.

The other great source of Christmas images flows from the triumph over winter darkness, which celebrates the year's turning at the solstice, promising the re-birth of light and the eventual coming of spring. Feasting, fire and light, and people coming together to celebrate the solstice and drive back the cold and fear of midwinter are all part of our holiday expectations. These are communal celebrations of family, clan and tribe. Loneliness is a curse that is felt as a failure at Christmas.

Christmas is a focus point for our joys and griefs. It glitters like a gemstone in the deep mine of human lives and imaginations. Like a crystal it magnifies, distorts, illuminates or splits human experience into story, poem, image and argument.

Because Christmas is an anniversary, each year cues memories of every other year. New experience is layered onto the old— for some creating a pearl, for some a cancer, as each year they remember old misery or pleasure and look ahead for more.

This collection of writings about Christmas shows human beings reflected in all their variety. Images glitter on the surface of a polished bowl or blur through a haze of tears. Storytellers give us characters that have courage, malice, patience, selfishness—their human strengths and frailties are reflected in their struggle with the effect of Christmas on their lives. Poets focus the lens of words to illuminate a piece of experience and give us new visions of a familiar season. Whether the characters in these stories are searching for the divine or the merely special, they come alive for us and may add a layer to our understanding of both the expected and the unexpected.

Betty Gibbs

Twas the Night

Cliff Burns

The rain finally falls on Christmas Eve and everyone stands at the window, holding strong drinks and smiling, not saying much, just watching. The streets get slick and shiny. Puddles form. Drinks are refreshed, cheeks flushed. The winking tree is reflected, refracted in the wet glass. Someone starts singing a carol, softly. No one else joins in and the voice trails off. The rain becomes sleet and everyone sucks in their breath. Let it snow, let it snow, let it snow. But the puddles just widen. One by one, they drift away from the window, leaving a small boy to continue the vigil. The lights are turned on, making it hard for him to see. He cups his hands against the glass. Harsh laughter behind him. The sound of something breaking. He doesn't look. If he waits long enough he's sure he'll see Santa, trailing after seven or maybe eight reindeer, soaked and shivering, laden with presents, falling like a stone.

Advent

Barb Howard

I got the advent calendar for filling up ten times at the gas station down the road. On top of this sparkly picture of kids playing in the snow there were twenty five little doors. I thought, Sarah being pregnant and all, that the calendar might help her count the days. Sarah said I should've used my voucher for more gas instead of a goddam calendar. But, all the same, I think she liked it. At least, the right paper door was open every day when I came home from work. Until December 19th. That was Sarah's due date and my last day of work before holidays. I called Sarah from work and said I was off for a few mugs of Christmas cheer with the boys. I remember her saying she'd break my balls if I came home boozed.

By the time I got home, Sarah had gone to bed. I could tell that she'd been pissed off at me 'cause the kitchen was real clean. Sarah gets to scrubbing when she's in a bad mood. I heated up a burrito in the microwave and hung over the sink to eat it. That's when I noticed that the December 19 door hadn't been opened. I stuffed the butt of the burrito in my mouth and picked up the calendar from the counter.

There was a mouse under December 19. Well, a cartoon mouse, with droopy eyes and a long red toque. I wondered how it was that mice in pictures got to be so cute. Real mice have those pointy brown teeth and hairless tails. Not that I'm scared of them. When Sarah and I moved into this house there was a whole family of mice living under our kitchen sink, crapping and eating macaroni bits off the s.o.s. pads. Sarah got rid of them.

I climbed into bed beside Sarah. She lay on her back, snoring like a well-oiled chainsaw. Sarah started snoring in October, about the same time she started wearing pajamas. Big red flannel pajamas that may as well have had a "keep out" sign on them. When I shoved her on her side she quit snoring. Maybe it was the eggnog acting, but as I lay there, one foot on the floor, one hand on the wall above my head, I heard a scraping sound in the next room, the one all done up for the baby. I had helped Sarah hang the little bear curtains in that room. It was tricky work 'cause I had to screw the rod into the top corner. In the end, the curtains hung a little crooked but, like I told Sarah, nothing a baby would notice.

The scraping got louder and pretty soon it sounded like a whole army of mice. I got up, pulled on my Stanfields and snuck into the baby's room. I flicked the light on. Nothing. Those little sneaks must've heard me coming. I was feeling all tense and sweaty so I went to the kitchen and got a beer and another burrito. When Sarah got up to pee, like she was doing a couple of times a night then, she stopped in the kitchen. I told her about the mice in the baby's room. She said so buy some traps, butthead.

I woke up early, after a bad sleep. You sure never know what you're getting with eggnog. I hung around the house drinking coffee and visiting the john until the stores opened. Then I took Bart, my '72 'Cuda, over to Canadian Tire. (I got Bart at last year's auction in Okotoks. Sarah was some mad, even after I explained about the re-built back end and original metallic paint.) I bought myself fifteen mousetraps. Back at the house, I set traps all over the baby's room and shut the door.

I asked Sarah if she was gonna open the calendar door for December 20. She said she didn't feel like it. She lay on the couch, surrounded by pillows, eating mandarin oranges. By noon she'd eaten about a carton and I got worried that all that citrus might do something to the baby. So I phoned my friend Jimmy who's got five kids. Jimmy said the only dangerous thing was horseback riding. That made me feel better, since we didn't have a horse, and I quit trying to put peels together to see how many oranges Sarah'd eaten. Still, it was almost like E.S.P. or something because when I opened December 20 on the calendar, there was a picture of an orange.

The next morning Sarah went straight to the couch and orange routine again so I figured the advent calendar had become my job. December 21 was a snowman. All the snowmen in our neighbourhood get their heads kicked in. Anyway, it reminded me that I hadn't shovelled the walk since last winter. I waited all morning to see if the sun was gonna shine and save me some work. No luck there. So in the late afternoon I got out my old metal shovel and started sweating. Halfway down the sidewalk the shovel snapped, right at the neck. I don't mind telling you that I was more than a bit glad to stop. My arms aren't the fork-lifts they used to be. I fired up Bart and drove to Canadian Tire for a new shovel. While I was there I strolled through the automotive section where a lady demonstrated shiny emergency blankets that fold into your glove compartment. I bought one, thinking it might be a good idea, especially once Sarah was driving around with a baby. Bart's

Advent

glove compartment was full of turtle wax and Armor All so I had to put the blanket under the seat.

December 22 was a Christmas candle burning with a churchy halo. I hadn't thought much about fire before. Not house fires. No way Sarah could escape through a window. She could barely get out of the shower stall. And those mice from the baby's room, they'd probably get a kick out of jamming a few doors or cutting the phone line. And Bart. What would happen to Bart?

I wrapped a roll of black tape round the bare wires of our toaster oven, replaced smashed bulbs on our Christmas lights and moved the barbecue propane tank from the kitchen to the alley. The barbecue was stolen last spring anyway. I revved up Bart and took a trip to Canadian Tire, charged twenty smoke detectors, three fire extinguishers and bought more black tape (I went a bit overboard on the toaster). When I got home Sarah said I should throw out the calendar because it was making me friggin' psycho. If anyone was friggin' psycho it was her. Moping around the house, looking in the 'fridge every twenty minutes, crying through A Charlie Brown Christmas on TV.

A present, all done in red and green paper, showed up under December 23. Now I knew this was a message for me since I still had to buy Sarah's Christmas gift. I know guys who'd get their missus a Thighmaster or a cook book. But it's like Sarah says, women like to be treated. In the automotive section at Canadian Tire I picked out some seat covers made out of wooden balls. The clerk said they'd be just the thing for Sarah's sore back. Then I got to thinking about Sarah driving with the new baby and icy roads and wet roads and traction. I decided to get new mag wheels for Bart.

December 24 was a fancy silver container that looked like a booze flask. I asked Sarah what the container had to do with

Barb Howard

Christmas. She said who the hell cares. But later, when I said I'd go buy another crate of oranges, she said maybe the flask was what one of the wisemen carried. I know all about the three wise guys, but I never can remember exactly what they brought the baby. Probably nothing dangerous. I mean, nothing with a skull and cross-bones on the label. Nothing like the DDT in the basement. (I bought a batch a few years back when the tent caterpillars were bad. Worked like a dream—so I bought extra.) Or the unopened paint and turpentine under the stairs. (When Sarah and I first got married I was gonna paint the house yellow. Buttercup yellow, Sarah called it. Buttercup. That was a while ago.)

I covered Bart's back seats with plastic (the trunk doesn't open too well in the winter), loaded up the DDT and paint and turpentine, and took it all down to the big dumpster behind Canadian Tire. When I got home I went into Sarah's cleaning cupboard and flushed everything like Draino down the toilet. There was a lot to be flushed and I had to do it slowly so's not to damage the pipes. It took most of the night. Sarah was a bit ticked, it being Christmas Eve and all. But, to be honest, it wasn't exactly a pleasure being in a room with her. I mean, she was real gassy. Probably from all those oranges.

Well I guess everyone knows what December 25 is on an advent calendar. I opened the twin doors and there sat a baby Jesus all pink-faced and golden-haired. Looked like a baby girl to me. Sometime, just for a surprise, they should put something other than Jesus there. Maybe a snowman or an orange. I got a surprise anyway 'cause Sarah gave me a new ball glove. Jimmy and the boys will be lookin' out this season. I gave Sarah her seat covers and showed her Bart's new mags. Sarah cooked us up bacon and waffles. Afterwards, I flicked on the TV for sports but all I could get was the Queen yacking on about this and that.

When I went to the kitchen to refill my coffee mug, Sarah was bent over, clutching the edge of the sink. The tap was spraying full blast. Suds spilled onto the floor. I asked Sarah if she knew the water was running and she said to shut the fuck up and get Bart started.

Sure enough, Sarah had the baby right on Christmas Day. I was there. Watched the whole thing. And I'll tell you, when all was done, that baby didn't look nothing like Jesus on the advent calendar. No sir. Even after they cleaned it up, that baby looked like it'd been in a bar brawl. Yellow face, bloated eyes, flat nose, purple hands. I thought it must be sick. Sarah said no, it just looked like me and then she laughed (like she used to before she got pregnant and started calling me butthead) and gave me a big kiss on the cheek.

Bart and I drove home alone since Sarah and the baby had to stay at the hospital. All the way I felt Sarah's kiss on my cheek and thought about that yellow mousy face in her arms. I parked Bart, unlocked the house, almost slipped on the wet kitchen floor, and tossed a burrito in the microwave. As the oven beeped I picked up the advent calendar and pushed it into the too-full garbage bin under the sink. Then I got out my power drill—those bear curtains needed fixing.

Barb Howard

Phone Calls

Alice Major

I
The phone calls came at Christmas, rarer
than the pomegranates the children had to share;
more costly, more improbable than strawberries
in December. They were often prearranged
by letters on thin blue paper with a Scottish stamp.
Our mother always neatly headed off the dash to answer.

"Oh George, so good to hear your voice. How's Kath?
And Iain—still doing well in school? And Alasdair?"

All of us cupped around the receiver, close
as a stocking round the apple in the toe.

"Och no, May, you know Alasdair. He'll work
no harder than he has to. Here he is."
"Happy Christmas, Auntie May.
           How's Uncle Willie?"
"Hi, Aunt Kath, I got a dress for Christmas."
"And don't you lassies sound like real wee Canadians now."
           "No we don't."

Then the operator's voice, like the taste
of an orange pip. "Your three minutes are up."

"George, George, we'll have to go. All this money."
"Aye, May, aye. Lovely to hear you all."

Goodbye, goodbye, a chorus of goodbyes. The hiss
of the Atlantic cut as cleanly as a cherry in a slice
of Christmas cake. Our mother would laugh and cry
together, and pick up tangerine peel
from the coffee table.

II
The phone calls came in the sombre hours
of the night, the heavy black receiver
lifted reluctantly.

"It's Dad, May. He went to the cottage hospital
this afternoon, insisted
on walking up himself. He just sat down
in the waiting room and passed away."

"Jean's gone, May. She went quickly
at the end. No, there's no point
in coming for the funeral. It's so expensive
and you've the bairns to think of."

The children wait at the end of the room,
can't imagine fathers, sisters dying,
can't comprehend mothers
crying this way.

19

Nellie's Vigil

Gary J. Langguth

The unshovelled no man's land between our houses is a rippling of brilliant white and deep shadow. Twice I've blundered through the crests of the powdery drifts. Shock at the soft flakes swishing against my knees, falling into my boots, melting around my bare ankles. I wish Nellie had left her back porch light on. I wish I had worn stockings. Now and then, the icy wind charges up my nightgown and freezes my backside. I can tell from the persistent quiver in my lower back that no matter how hot Nellie's stoves are burning tonight, I'll never get warm.

It's my own fault. Running between houses at four in the morning in nothing but my ratty pink nightie and old winter coat. I must be getting senile. I've got half a mind to turn around and head back under the covers beside Pat. But I know Nellie will be up waiting and I won't let her down. Not tonight. Besides, it's only a couple more feet to her back steps and the old wicker mat—and thank God, the key's under it!

Teeth chattering, I turn the key in the lock and let myself in as quietly as I can. George has never been roused by my annual visits and I'm not about to break with tradition now. I doubt the old bird would appreciate the disturbance.

I slip out of Pat's old leather boots (which I see I didn't bother to zip) and step into a clod of slush. It burns my heels.

I can almost hear Momma crying, "Katie, Katie, Katie—what am I going to *do* with you?" I've been doing things like this for fifty-eight years, and now, as I stand in my big sister's unlit porch, my back shaking, my ass numb, my toes wet and cold, I'm finally convinced that I am too old for this sort of thing.

The door swings back on its hinges, slowly revealing Nellie's kitchen—dark, quiet, and full of white ghosts, which turn out to be George's thermal underwear hanging on the line over the wood stove. Its smooth white belly feels cool beneath my palm. The evening fire must have died hours ago.

Nellie seems to have abandoned the place. There's no golden loaf of bread cooling on the stove top, no store-bought mocha cakes on the table, and not a sound from the kettle when I shake it. But I know my sister is expecting me. I've been making these early morning visits for twenty years.

I steal a glance in the direction of George's room. The door is ajar, enough so I can see the old fart: a grey-haired mound facing the wall, buried beneath a heap of quilts and wool blankets. An agitated groan rises from the bedding as it adjusts itself, then silence. Sleeping off another one, I suppose—although my sister would never admit it.

My thoughts are interrupted by the whir of a fan and the flapping of flames. Sounds of warmth, coming from the oil stove in the dining room. I tear off my water-jewelled coat and pad toward the sounds at a pace hastened by the cool linoleum under my bare feet. As soon as I step into the dining room, however, my progress is impeded by something large and wooden. A chair, the one at the head of the great hardwood table.

The table is much too big for this room. Everything else in here—the eight high-back chairs, the bulky china cabinet, George's rocker with the grey flannelette blanket slung over it, the new RCA (a colour floor model), and the oil stove (a Fawcett)—is huddled about its massive maple rectangularity, like a crowd of beggars desperate for a place to stay. I've lost track of how many times Nellie and I have served Christmas dinner at this table. We always had quite a crowd, because Nellie and I had eighteen kids and grandkids between us. I can remember setting this one and the chrome set in the kitchen two and three times and even then a few of the grandkids got stuck with George's rocker. And in the middle of it all would be Nellie, decked out in her red and green apron, speeding around the room. Followed by George, red-faced and a bit amorous from a nip of white lightning. Nellie would force her plump figure around the corners of the table, deal out a scoop of mashed potatoes to one of the kids, and then, almost breathless from laughter, she'd shake her big wooden spoon at George, call him a fool, and then she'd be off again. The two of them giggling madly like the grandkids.

The table is bare tonight. Nellie and I don't expect anyone this year. Jim and his three hellions are away (thank God!), Grace moved into her new flat in the South End so she won't be here, and it looks like none of my kids will be home either. Not even Troy. It's going to be just the four of us: Nellie, old George, Pat, and me.

I drape my coat over the offending chair and, manoeuvring it so I don't scrape the legs, I pull it nearer the stove. By the faint orange glow coming from its gut, however, I read that it's only set to one. Hell will freeze over before I get warm in here.

I flip it up to four. It may take an hour or so (and some of the old fart's oil), but it'll be toasty in here by the time I leave.

Nellie's Vigil

That done, I turn from the stove and squeeze my way through to the parlour. Once my toes touch the cool fuzziness of the carpet, my eyes dart to the darkest corner of the room, between the big front window and the smaller one adjacent to it. Given form by loops of snowy garland and a few glistening strands of tinsel, the five-foot fir gradually emerges from the shadows: short, fat, and so densely branched that there seems to be a certain softness, a certain roundness to it. And, in all of its rich, needled darkness, I notice something else: an emptiness.

I spot the reason for this on the coffee table: a small stack of unopened cardboard cartons. Ornaments. From the bargain basement at the Five and Ten. Twenty-seven cents apiece, if I remember correctly.

En route to the table, I nearly trip. On what, I'm not certain. I can't believe how damn dark it is in this house. Once, lights the colour of sunny egg yolks outlined the kitchen window. Scarlet streamers rocketed across the dining room ceiling. A set of electric candles with big orange bulbs lit up the picture window. The Charlie Brown evergreen and both stoves burned brightly all night. And every year there was a lunch—a pot of tea, a bit of savory onion dressing, something.

And tonight? On the coffee table, I spy a bowl of rock-hard striped satin mix and a plate of sugar-edged lemon wedges. No lunch, no lights, no nothing. Just Nellie, sitting by the window, and me. And the half-decorated tree.

Humbug.

I pull a dusty cover off one of the boxes, slip my finger through a loop of string and raise my hand into the dim light filtering through the window. An ancient sugar-coated snowball appears. I watch it for a moment, a tiny world spinning in the night. Then, with my free hand, I bend one of the stiff upper branches toward

Gary J.Langguth

me. Needles shower onto the wrapped gifts below. I place the ornament on the dry twig, among the tangled maze of glazed blue bulbs and rippled foil reflectors. As I do this, I glimpse the features of the angel perched at the top. In this light, she appears not rosy-cheeked but deathly pale, not solemn but sad, with eyes shut not in prayer but perhaps in an effort to blink away tears.

Eager to avoid the scrutiny of the dispirited crown, I open two more cartons and resume my task. Armed with a few lime-striped candy canes and some glass baubles that resemble frozen teardrops, I do my best to fill in the empty spots. In time, I fall with a sigh onto the couch. Beside Nellie.

For the past twenty years, she has kept her vigil, here on the rust-coloured couch, nearest the draught of the picture window. Bathed in the blue of the streetlight, she meditates on snow-dusted Westmorland Road and the whitened gravel path which wanders among the oak and maple trees and vanishes into the depths of Fernhill Cemetery.

On her lap rests one of the leather-bound family albums, opened to a faded page. Taped to it is a tiny photograph. A black and white cardboard square, creased and print-smeared, with a fair-sized chunk missing from the bottom left corner.

It's the only one in the book. Before he left, Jack ripped all the memories out and tossed them into the wood stove; Nellie found this one on the kitchen floor that night. It's become something of a relic. It's her only picture of him.

Nellie has shown it to me hundreds of times; I don't need to see it. When I think of my nephew, I see the hyperactive six-year-old on that treasured scrap, captured in mid-bounce beneath that year's scrawny fir.

It troubles me to look at him. So pale and thin. Despite Nellie's best efforts, he never looked like he got enough to eat. And his eyes, bulging from his tiny face. They look not at you, but through you, beyond you. Obviously fixed on something else, somewhere else. I find his smile equally unsettling. For some unknown reason, Jack always smiled with clenched teeth. As if he expected some great disaster.

Maybe he did.

I always wondered what was wrong with him. What illness he was born with. I sensed it in him the first time I held him in Nellie's cramped two-room flat on Prince Edward Street. I remember how he trembled in my arms.

I still wonder what it was that made my sister sit up nights crying. What it was that etched deep lines into her forehead and cheeks. Whatever it was, it was something she and George would never speak of. Sometimes, late at night, Pat and I whispered about it, but we never asked.

Now, Nellie waits and prays quietly in the window.

I study her wrinkled hands, peppered with age spots. Her beads, dangling below, click slightly as she contemplates her own sorrowful mystery.

She must be worn out from midnight mass. At her age, I'm not surprised.

I half-expected her to stay home tonight. But once again, after the last verse of "Hark, the Herald Angels Sing," after the great organ fell silent, after the aisles emptied and the last murmuring parishioners spilled out into the storm, I found her. In the right nave, kneeling on the stone-cold floor before the Pieta. Looking up at Mary cradling the body of her dead Son, at the mother supporting her Child's head in one hand and holding His right arm in the other like a big bouquet of flowers.

Despite George's protests and my best efforts to dissuade her, she lingers there every year, still hoping he will show up.

Gary J. Langguth

I always hate leaving her, but tonight I felt especially bad. And a bit guilty.

If only I hadn't talked Pat into midnight mass...

But I had been set on going to the Cathedral. The Cathedral of the Immaculate Conception, at the top of the hill on Waterloo Street. Big and airy, with great arches, towering pillars, flying buttresses, huge plaster apostles staring down on the altar blanketed in white linen, beeswax candles flickering in gold stands, dozens of red and white potted poinsettias, and row after row of oak pews packed with the chilled and the well-bundled.

Pat and I were late, of course. As we squeezed into the last pew, my eyes picked out a man at the back, weighted down with a battered beige suitcase. I caught him pacing, fidgeting about the holy water font. A young man, in his early forties. Tall and skinny, as if he'd been tied to a rack and stretched. He wore a pair of navy work pants at least four sizes too big, a grey wool sweater with an inky stain on the front, and a shabby black overcoat. Obviously from the Salvation Army.

A bum, I thought, at first. Then he stopped and ran a filthy hand through his greasy black mop, so that I finally got a good look at his face. His chalky white face, dark with sleep and stubble. His big black eyes, glassy and bloodshot. And within them, behind them, something not quite right.

Something familiar.

Animated by foolish curiosity, I found myself following his every move. Around the font, over to Mr. LeBlanc and the other ushers, back, toward the table stacked with the weekly bulletins and missalettes, back, over to the ushers, and back again. And as I watched, every now and then, his mouth twitched and flashed two rows of white teeth at the ushers.

Nellie's Vigil

I thought he might take a seat, but he didn't. By the time the choir sang out the opening of "O Come, O Come Emmanuel" and the mitred bishop bearing the plaster likeness of Baby Jesus appeared, he was gone.

I didn't have the heart to mention him to Nellie.

My sister completes her fifth decade and then, with a shaky hand, blesses herself. Her lips mouth the words: "In the name of the Father. And of the Son. And of the Holy Spirit."

Beside her lies the unopened gift. A round package, still wrapped in white tissue, still tied with the same crimson ribbon. On the yellowed tag, still written in smudged ink: "Merry Christmas Jack, Love Mum."

God only knows what's in it.

Nellie fingers the tag briefly, then places it beneath the tree for the twentieth time.

The ritual complete, she settles back onto the couch, presses her calloused palm against the glittering pane, then peers through the melted impression.

For twenty years I've been here to hold her when she shakes with secret tears, haunted by the ragged youngster in the snapshot. And right now, as Nellie leans ever closer to the shrinking wet circle, I am glad I braved the elements.

All is calm and quiet in the Sullivan house.

"I thought sure he'd come home tonight," she whispers at last. And she looks at me, through eyes which, though baggy and ringed from want of rest, are surprisingly dry and bright and—at peace. And with absolute certainty, she says "Tonight, I *felt* him there."

For an eternity, she studies me, carefully, thoughtfully. I desperately want to blink away her smile, but cannot.

I can see the two of them standing on the windy corner of King and Charlotte on that Christmas Eve so long ago. Nellie,

Gary J. Langguth

27

armed with brown bags of groceries from the Dominion Store and that small secret parcel, buttoning her son's coat and waving at him as she crosses the street, heading in the direction of the Five and Ten, the Old City Market, and ultimately, the Cathedral. And Jack, then twenty-two, carrying his own bags and his own secrets, flashing his smile and waving back as he shifts his weight from one foot to the other beneath the streetlight. I can almost hear him chanting, "I'll meet you there, Mumma. I'll be there, Mumma. I'll be there."

At last, Nellie gets up, yawns, stretches, and leaves the parlour. I hold my breath until I hear the groan of bed-springs in the distance, then move over and take her place near the window.

With the warmth of my hand, I renew the peep-hole in the frost. Through the frigid pane, I feel the power of the winds that shake the house, shift the white dunes outside, and make the snow-spirits wither across the deserted road. When a glittering tear dribbles down the glass, I remove my wet palm, ready to keep watch for Jack, Grace, Troy, all our children.

Sunrise is still hours away.

Nellie's Vigil

A Kind of Christmas Poem

John B. Lee

We must not speak of how the snow
was fudged here and there
with the dung of dog.
Nor how the tar-winged crows
beaked a road-kill in the halo of headlights.
Not how half-eaten fish-gilled oranges
flapped their rinds in the trash.
Nor how the drunk nubbed his whiskered lip
on a bottle mouth
then spat
the smashed cricket of his phlegm
in the street.
Nor how the father grumbled
out of work.
Nor how the young girl
turned a trick.
Nor how the river grew glassy
where the commerce
rolled like crack smoke
high above the factory wall
while some slept huddled
like a window-cleaner's rags
where they blew their brittle fingers
so they pulsed
with heat-ejaculated pain.

Nor of humans dying in hospitals
piping and
peeping like the unintelligible syllables
of dolphins and whales
or hissing in sleep
like campers' lanterns
their heartbeats raging
like an interrupted writer
and all the awful
accumulated agonies of loss, regret,
disappointment and spoiled revenge.
For this is Christmas
time to prettify our wounds
as if the shepherds were not crude,
and babies did not cack, stars roar, camels bark,
and wise men pontificate
an audience until it slept, despaired,
departed, disillusioned,
broken-hearted.

A Kind of Christmas Poem

Christmas On
the Other Hand

Sybil Shaw-Hamm

C hristmas was to be rearranged. Alice first heard about it when Lenny dropped by after work. "Mother," Lenny said, "Shirley and I plan to go up to Swan River for Christmas this year."

"You what! And leave me here alone on Christmas Day."

"We never have, have we, Mother? Not once in the nine years of our marriage. Well, this year Shirley needs to go home."

"Never," Alice said.

"It's only fair."

"Fair! You know something to tell me about fair. Shirley's mother has a whole family...a husband...five children...grandchildren...alive."

"Please Mother, don't start."

"And just what, pray tell, do you suggest I do all by myself on Christmas Day?"

Lenny sighed and brushed a hand through his thinning hair. "I don't know. Maybe you could ask someone in for dinner? Maybe you could go out to church."

Afterward Alice will likely tease Lenny. "It was you who suggested it, you know."

Not that Lenny wasn't a good son. Alice knew he was, except for his nagging about her going back to church. Yet the religion business wasn't exactly Lenny's fault. Alice started him off that way herself, years ago. "As dependable as a good clock," Alice used to say about how her family attended to the church. Then nine years ago, on the highway between Swan River and Winnipeg, after Lenny's wedding, Alice declared churches useless; she declared religion null and void. And the name that once slipped so easily off her tongue she now refused to say. For God, as far as Alice was concerned, had been obliterated, along with a mother and a daughter and a husband when the car went up in smoke. Would Alice ever go back to church again? Not on her life.

What Alice did consider, however, was inviting someone over for dinner. Let's see: she thought: Charlotte and Harry are away to Texas; Irene has gone to spend Christmas with a brother in Saskatoon; Agnes and Marjorie, of course, have no time for their old friends anymore; no doubt they'll spend the day at work, at the Refuge House, with a bunch of strangers.

"No one," Alice reported to Lenny and Shirley.

Nevertheless, Christmas was rearranged.

December twenty third: The turkey was cooked. Lenny and Shirley came over in the late afternoon. They ate. They exchanged gifts. They watched a Christmas special on channel six. "Have a happy Christmas, Mother," they said to Alice when they left.

December twenty fourth: Most of the day Alice sat by the phone waiting for the call that would tell her Lenny and Shirley were...well...were safe...one way or the other. By the time Lenny phoned that evening Alice was so tired that as soon as she hung up the phone she went straight off to bed.

Christmas morning: Alice awoke, or she half woke, and stretched a hand across the cold bedsheet and found the empty space...no husband...no daughter... no mother...no God. Found them dead, all over again, after nine years. She remembered fresh, like it had just happened. And hot rage rolled down into Alice's lonesome soul.

"It was the lonesomeness that drove me to it," Alice will likely tell Shirley and Lenny when they ask her why she went.

As Alice neared the old stone church she heard voices rolling out, "Merry Christmas, Merry Christmas." As she slid into the back row she heard the choir singing "Angels from the realms of glory."

After the benediction Alice leaned toward the pew in front of her. Much to her own relief, instead of saying a last minute prayer as she feared she was about to do, she tapped the shoulder of the woman who sat there. "Merry Christmas," Alice said to the woman.

"Chriz Miz," the woman replied, her black ringlets springing from a golden turban, her white toothed smile springing from between red lips.

Some refugee, Alice thought: some lonesome soul wandering in a strange land.

On her way home from church Alice saw the reflection of her own lips in the window at Whitefield Drugs; she formed the word "Chriz Miz," which was why she wasn't as surprised as she might have been when they bumped together.

"Zcuzie," the woman said and held the teetering Alice steady with her hands.

"Have I hurt you?" Alice wanted to know.

"Chriz Miz," the woman said grinning at Alice and pointing back toward the church.

Alice will likely tell Lenny and Shirley about the woman. She'll defend herself. "Not exactly a stranger," she'll say. "We'd met before."

"My name is Alice."

"My name iz Gayuma."

33

Sybil Shaw-Hamm

"Gayuma, if you have no other plans, no other place to go, come home with me for Christmas dinner." Alice will likely try to explain that she was surprised too, to hear herself say those words.

As the two women stood side by side on the cold street, Alice feared the uselessness of words. She plucked a figurative fork out of the frosty air and began to eat. "Come." Alice pointed to the apartment block peaking above the row of buildings in front of them. Alice took two steps forward along the icy sidewalk. Gayuma stayed where she was. "Come, come." Alice beckoned and reached back for the other woman's arm. Alice teetered. Gayuma grabbed her. "Come," Alice said when she had Gayuma's arm firmly tucked under her own. "We'll have Christmas dinner at my apartment."

At the apartment Alice placed on the table the food left over from the dinner with Lenny and Shirley: Jerusalem artichoke soup, noisettes of lamb in plum sauce, cold roast turkey, sausage turkey dressing, parsnip and potato puree, stuffed Spanish onions, an avocado salad and a platter of various pickles.

Gayuma stared at the table. "Iz Chriz Miz in thiz country to eat az much az you can?"

Alice laughed. "I suppose it is," she said, thinking the question was answered. They sat down and ate as much as they could.

"Aliz," Gayuma said when the meal ended and the two women settled in the living room with their tea. "Aliz, what really iz thiz Chriz Miz thing in your country?

"Could it be to eat with a stranger, maybe? I juz come here and the lights and pretty things say to myself, 'Aheh, thiz Chriz Miz thing iz for the market place, the shops, the cash.' But then I get my idea mezzed up at church. Now, you mezz it up too."

"Well, let's see, Gayuma. What can I tell you about Christmas?

Well, I'd say, it's a holiday really. Yes, a holiday, when families and friends get together."

"You have a family?"

"One son and one daughter-in-law. Gone to Swan River."

"Thiz River iz far away."

"Yes. Far away."

"My homeland, too, iz far away."

Alice, with some embarrassment over the comparison of distances, was quick to ask Gayuma about her family.

"None. Not any more."

Alice offered her more tea.

"She just wouldn't give up," Alice will likely tell Lenny and Shirley when they come home. " 'Aliz,' she kept at me, 'Aliz, what iz thiz Chriz Miz thing?' "

"Look," Alice finally said to Gayuma, laying two hands palm up on the couch between them. "See this hand." Alice wiggled her right hand. "On this hand is food and family and friends and gifts and lights and singing and parties and celebrations. And, yes, the market place, as you say, and the cash."

"Iz Chriz Miz?"

"Yes. On one hand it is. On the other hand," and Alice wiggled her left hand, "...on the other hand is something else."

"What?"

Alice felt her mouth go dry.

Gayuma waited.

Alice tried. "It's..."

Gayuma waited.

"It's G... It's the angels and the manager and the stars and..."

Gayuma waited.

"It's Go... It's the cattle that low and the wise people who come and the shepherds who care..."

Sybil Shaw-Hamm

"Thiz iz Chriz Miz?"

"Not exactly."

"Well I had to say, didn't I?" Alice will likely say this later to excuse her broken oath of obliteration. "I could hardly leave the poor soul in a new country, alone, drifting about, thinking Canadians make Christmas into so much puff."

Beside Gayuma on the couch Alice wiggled her other hand. "God lives here," she said. "We have Christmas once a year to say we still believe God lives here among us."

"God?" Gayuma pointed upward.

Alice nodded.

Gayuma pointed at Alice's hand. "God?"

Alice nodded.

The laugh, when it began, began deep in Gayuma's chest, a slight hiccup, a sigh, a moving giggle, an escaping chuckle, a roar.

"Zcuzie," Gayuma said, and straighted herself up, straightened up the turban which had slipped sideways on her head, placed her hands together in her lap, pressed her top lip firmly down. "Zcuzie, Aliz, but Chriz Miz iz God on that hand?"

Alice reached for Gayuma's hand and turned it palm up. "And there, on that hand too. And here. And everywhere in this world. God is with us no matter where we are or what is going on."

Gayuma and Alice looked at each other. They looked down at the hands.

"Iz true, Aliz. God right here between uz two women?"

"It's what I believe. Yes."

"Iz good, Aliz. I like."

"Is good, Gayuma. I like too."

"Chriz Miz, Alice."

"Christmas, Gayuma."

Later, Lenny will phone from Swan River. Alice will tell him she went out in the morning for a walk. She'll tell him she met a friend by the corner of Whitefield's Drug Store and invited her home for dinner.

"Did you enjoy the day, Mother?"

"Lenny, my dear," Alice will say, "I think I could go for it every second year."

"Are you alone now, Mother?"

"You might call it alone," Alice will say with a smile, and she'll add, "You two have a good holiday now. Seasons greetings to Shirley's folks. We'll see you both in a few days. Happy Christmas, Lenny."

And Lenny, who hasn't been wished happiness in nine years, will know a mother's Christmas gift when he hears it.

Sybil Shaw-Hamm

Mother and Child

Dianne Linden

my Daughter and I walked out late on Christmas Eve.
we followed our usual pattern,
down the road that runs along the ravine, then
up a little hill to houses, sidewalks, lights again.

I was crying by the time we got to the top. it
could have been hormonal, or just the time of year.
you'll make your face colder if you cry, she said and
that made me do it more so she put her arm through mine:
held herself against me as we walked along.

two kids drove up behind us in a car that rattled like a tank.
hey you Dykes, they yelled. get the fuck off this road!
their car spun its wheels, tractionless for a moment
on the icy pavement. my Daughter turned to face them.
you Jerks, she called as they sped away. this is my Mother.
for Christ's sake, I'm out walking with my Mother!

I began to laugh. we both began to laugh,
holding each other in the snowy lane:
to think anyone would take us for lovers,
with Christmas only moments away.

The American Hotel

Wynne Edwards

I t could have been any of a number of Christmases; maybe the little girl was four or five, maybe a little older or younger. Sometime during that Christmas Day the father, who was a pleasant drunk and not uneasy to be with, discovered his last bottle was nearly empty. He bundled the little girl into the battered Plymouth and drove the few blocks over gravel to the main street of the town.

The air was crisp but it was not so cold as some Christmases on the Canadian prairie. The little girl would be warm enough and was happy enough to go. The few presents under the tree had been opened early in the morning and the excitement that had sustained her for weeks had faltered. The older brother had gone sledding with a friend. The mother was tight-lipped and uncommunicative as she prepared Christmas dinner for the four of them.

At a three-story brick structure with the unlikely name of the American Hotel, the father halted the car. As he stepped out, he smiled and told the little girl he would be back soon. She knew from experience this was not true but she smiled back. It was not unusual for her to sit in the car outside a hotel beer parlour. Often her brother was with her and they would fight;

it was better to be alone.

The inside of the hotel was a place of mystery to the little girl. She did not know that today the beer parlour would be closed, and that the hotel desk clerk would be persuaded because it was Christmas, to sell the father a bottle of rye whiskey, to share a drink from it in the office behind the desk.

Waiting in the car, the little girl hummed softly, sang the few words of Silent Night that she knew. Then she played with her new doll, Sarah Jane, pretended she was Sarah Jane's mother, alternately loving and admonishing her for her imaginary transgressions. She was almost unaware of the brown bristles of the Plymouth's upholstery, rubbing and reddening her thighs in the space where brown, gartered stockings and cotton underpants didn't quite meet. She was accustomed now to the lingering gasoline smell that together with the dusty odour of the upholstery had made her sick when her father first brought the old car home.

At a pause in her play she stretched her neck to see out the side window of the Plymouth. The street was empty, as were the single-storey shops with their two-storey false fronts. White's Department Store, which had ladies' ready-to-wear at the top of an oiled wood staircase, was dark, with its Venetian window blinds lowered. The butcher shop, which usually had trays of meat displayed in the windows and sawdust on the floor, was bare today. Even the Roxy Theatre was dark. The street was familiar yet unfamiliar. The little girl preferred to play with Sarah Jane. The sun, now low in the west, reflected on her dark hair and on the stiff and shiny blonde hair of Sarah Jane, warming their heads.

The little girl was startled by a tap on the car window beside her and was momentarily frightened to see a round, smiling face just inches away from hers, with only the window glass between them. A young woman was peering in, smiling tentatively. She indicated with a circling motion of her hand that the child should open the window. The little girl hesitated, then struggled with the crank until the glass lowered a short distance.

The young woman was stocky, with light brown hair, long and tied back, which curled in a frizzy way. Her face had a pink, scrubbed look. She wore a red, handknit sweater with a brown coat pulled over it, heavy brown stockings and stout brown shoes tied with cotton laces. In spite of her matronly appearance, the young woman standing next to the car was little more than a child herself.

She spoke to the little girl in thick, accented English, "I speak very small English...You talk to me?" The little girl remained silent, unsure how to respond but no longer frightened.

"I work here..." the young woman pointed to the nearby American hotel, "...maid. You live this city?" She struggled with the "th" sound.

The little girl smiled; she was old enough to know that the small town that bordered her life was not called a city.

"I come from Deutschland...Germany. How old...?" She gestured toward her and the little girl automatically held up the appropriate number of fingers.

"Me...I...sechzehn...sixteen. Pretty baby...," the young woman pointed a rough-skinned finger at Sarah Jane.

The child eagerly twisted the window crank until the glass was lowered completely. Sarah Jane was held up for inspection. The young woman took the proffered doll and examined it admiringly before returning it to the arms of the little girl.

When the father returned, carrying his partially empty bottle in a plain brown bag, the young woman was still there talking

41

Wynne Edwards

earnestly, partly in English, partly in German. The little girl was nodding politely, answering the young woman's questions. The father also spoke to her, wished her a Merry Christmas. They said goodbye, and as the father and daughter drove off, the young woman waved after them until they turned the corner at the end of the block and she could no longer see them.

On the short drive home the little girl chattered to her father. Why was the young woman alone at Christmas? Where were her mummy and daddy? Did Santa Claus come to her here or only in Germany? How far away was Germany? Her father smiled at his talkative child and she smiled back. She didn't find his drinking offensive. It was when he was most friendly and when he gave her money she wouldn't normally get. It did make her nervous because of her mother's anger. She was afraid of her mother's anger, which seethed inside her, bubbling just below her skin. Even a tender touch at the wrong time could cause it to come bursting to the surface.

The little girl momentarily forgot what the mother's reaction might be, as she and her father made a plan to go back and find the lonely young woman. To bring her home to their Christmas table which was small, but big enough for one more. The child would give the young woman one of her Christmas presents, the small glass bottle of Jergens hand lotion. They agreed to go to their house first since it was getting late. Reassure the mother they were all right and coming home soon. Then drive back the few blocks to collect the young woman.

When they entered the small kitchen that smelled of roasted turkey and mincemeat pies, the mother was waiting, her face grim. Christmas dinner had been ready for an hour. The potatoes were cold, the turkey dry. The four of them ate the dinner served on the fancy paper tablecloth. The mother sat quietly, eating small

The American Hotel

bites slowly, tears standing in her eyes. The older brother, who was growing rapidly that year, attacked the food on his plate vigorously without looking up. The father ate and talked, made small jokes, tried to invoke a spirit which had long since died. The little girl responded to the jokes with little murmurs, tiny giggles.

The highway no longer passes through the small town, which used to be the stop-off place for American tourists going to the Calgary Stampede. There are a handful of stores and one grain elevator left. White's Department Store, the butcher shop, the Roxy Theatre, all are closed. The young German woman could be "Oma" to grandchildren older than the little girl outside the American Hotel. The family: the father, the mother, the older brother and the little girl, moved away from the town a few years later. That Christmas and the others like it were forgotten.

Wynne Edwards

White

Jacqueline Bell

He got a quarter for Christmas
was told to buy his own present
down at the general store in Clyde.
Had to walk there first though
five miles in freezing cold.

We were never told this; we heard
lectures, we'd mimic the gestures
they were so familiar, mouthing
the words, angry, behind his back.

How lucky we were,
he'd walked miles to school in deep snow.
His resentment, an ice-berg we broke ourselves against.
It spread farther, deeper than we could.

The lectures made us feel greedy
for wanting what we shouldn't.
He felt it too, a longing
for what a quarter couldn't buy,
or even a house full of quarters.
Something fading, out of reach
a blurred figure in a blizzard.

In later years he couldn't understand
what was missing in our house.
Christmases with trees and presents and turkey.
A family of scarecrows, stuffed full
but empty. Keeping the world away so
no one could see our shameful hunger.

Maybe we could have felt luckier
if he'd told us the real story.
How sometimes they didn't have enough to eat
or just how long that walk was
when breath froze on hair and
everywhere was white.

Christmas
in the
Country

Syr Ruus

She wasn't looking forward to this visit. It would be good to see the grandchildren, of course, and Jane *was* her only child. They had been on good terms until Michael came along. Then everything changed. Jane became resentful and evasive. When Meredith asked about anything personal, she would answer, but never look her directly in the eye.

Meredith sighs loudly and presses her lips together, leaning back against the faded plush.

First her daughter. Then her husband. Gone. Stayed until the child was raised, then left to live his own life. She could hardly mourn him, for he was already living with another woman before he died. But she mourned for Jane, still alive and claiming to be happily married, though Meredith doubted it. Michael had long hair and no steady job. The artistic type. Jane taught school to support him and the kids. Even when they were babies she had to be the breadwinner in the family. It wasn't right. She could have done better. But she would never admit it, especially to her mother. Jane didn't accept criticism well. She could never face up to a mistake.

Meredith sighs again and looks absently out the bus window at the soggy, gray city. Not like Christmas was supposed to be. Across the parking lot she sees a skinny girl in tight jeans and pink parka, the fake fur matted and yellow around the hood, dragging a small boy behind her. His short legs in baggy corduroy trousers move twice as fast as hers to keep up, but still she keeps tugging him forward.

"You goin to Western Shore?" she asks the driver.

"No," he says. "This here's the Express. We don't stop in them little towns."

The two of them stand in the icy drizzle looking up through the open door.

"The house is right beside the highway," she says finally, "with a white picket fence around it. You can't miss it. Will you just stop so's we can get off thar?"

The driver considers a moment, looking at the girl and then at the kid.

"Yeah," he says slowly. "I guess we can do that. But you gotta pay full fare anyhow. And you gotta tell me when to stop."

She has no suitcase or anything, just a shoulder bag and the kid.

They pick the seat right in front of Meredith and at the first traffic light, the kid starts in: "Are we thar yet, Ma?" he whines, standing up on the seat and pressing his face against the window.

"No, not for a while yet," says the mother, keeping her voice low, though it seems obvious to Meredith that she is a type more used to shouting.

"Look at that, Ma," the kid hollers, pointing. "What's that thar, Ma?"

"Shush. You gotta be quiet on the bus," she says.

"What fur, Ma?" he asks.

She has no answer to that one.

She seems to be no more than eleven herself, until you look closely. Then the dead ends of her dyed hair and the sallow skin over her cheekbones give her away.

"When we gonna get thar, Ma?" he whines again after a space of two or three minutes.

It nearly drives Meredith crazy, the whining. Why did they have to pick a seat right in front of her? The bus was still half empty when she got on, its motor idling softly, the driver busy outside filling the luggage compartment with packages. Meredith had taken a taxi to the station early. She didn't know how she'd manage by herself with the two heavy suitcases, one of them full of presents. She wasn't used to traveling in buses. There was no reason they couldn't have driven to the city to pick her up, no reason at all, she thinks resentfully, but she has learned over the years not to speak her mind. It would only lead to a big argument, the same old accusations, and spoil Christmas for them all. As it was, she always felt uncomfortable at Jane's, with Michael there. Unwelcome. The kids would latch on to her right away of course, Jenny and Mike Jr., eager to see what she had brought them. They'd have to wait until Christmas morning, but she might be allowed to give them at least one of their gifts early.

As she thinks of her grandchildren, her face softens. An expression close to a smile plays around her lips. She is caught unawares by the boy, standing backwards on the seat, staring at her out of somber dark eyes.

Before the impudent brat has a chance to speak she fixes her face to its accustomed severity, opens her purse and pretends to be searching for something. It works. Soon the boy tires of looking and settles into his seat. Not for long. When the bus stops at the next light, he scrambles to his feet again.

"Are we thar now, Ma?" he yells. "Is this the country, Ma?"

"No," she says. "Hush. We got a long ways to go yet."

Christmas in the Country

But the kid won't hush.

"What's Nanny's house like then?" he asks, tugging at her sleeve.

"Nice," she tells him. "I ain't never been there myself, but I'm certain it's nice. Houses is nice in the country."

That seems to satisfy him.

Soon the traffic thins out. The bus pulls onto the highway and picks up speed. All that can be heard is the clack of windshield wipers, the steady drone of the motor, and muffled voices from the crowd in back. The little boy must be asleep.

But now that everything is quiet and the boy no longer a nuisance, Meredith wants him awake and talking. Was there really someone waiting, she wonders. Was there truly a Nanny in Western Shore in a house surrounded by a white picket fence? She looks out the window at a gray landscape punctuated by scraggly evergreens clutching at thin rocky soil. Not many houses to relieve the monotony of the view. None with a fence. Clumps of withered yellow grass the only patches of colour.

Across the aisle sits a youngish woman, prissy and spinsterish, black sensible shoes set neatly side by side on the muddy floor. Every once in a while, she underlines something in a small volume, then gazes off into space. Meredith tries her best to get a glimpse of the title. Probably a religious tract of some kind, judging by the woman's demeanour. Perhaps she is a nun. Since they have stopped wearing the habit, one can never be sure.

In front of her sits an unattractive girl with greasy brown hair and a bad complexion, reading also. A tabloid. Meredith can make out a red headline predicting dire events in the New Year. The girl's attention seems to wander to the delicate pink rose wrapped in cellophane that she has placed on the empty seat beside her. Several times she picks it up to sniff it. Who could it be for, Meredith wonders.

49

Syr Ruus

The bus is almost full, most of the passengers being college students returning home for the holidays. They sit together in the back, their duffel bags carelessly flung on the racks above. Meredith hears their faint laughter and imagines talk of parties, past and yet to come. She feels like crying. Somehow, somewhere, life had passed her by. Every Christmas she feels it. She always tried to convince herself that life was full. She kept herself busy. She had many friends, her bridge club, her volunteer work. But maybe, after all, it was quite empty.

All these other passengers had somewhere to go, something they looked forward to. What did she have? A daughter who no longer loved her. A son-in-law she despised. Grandchildren she really didn't know, who were only interested in the gifts she brought.

"Are we thar yet, Ma?" the little boy's voice asks again in her mind, though the questioner himself is now sound asleep, drool oozing out of the side of his slack and peaceful mouth.

Meredith wants to doze off herself in the stuffy warmth of the bus, yet a strange compulsion keeps her wide awake, looking out the window for a house with a white picket fence. The bus driver seems to have assumed the same responsibility judging by the number of times his concerned blue eyes glance back into the rear-view mirror.

Suddenly the bus slows and then stops altogether on the shoulder of the highway. All the passengers become attentive as the driver turns around.

"You never did tell me to stop," he says accusingly. "We're a-ways past Western Shore now."

"I didn't see no picket fence," she whines into the silence. "What am I supposed to do?"

He thinks hard before he answers.

"We're not that far past yet." he says. "Maybe you oughta get off here. Before we go any farther. There's a service station up the hill. You could call someone. Maybe they would come and pick you up."

We all gape at her as she moves down the aisle, pulling on the little boy still rosy and muddled from sleep. The bus door opens with a hiss.

"Is this the country, Ma?" the kid is shouting as they disappear down the steps into the cold.

Barely visible in the gray mist, a tiny pink figure drags a smaller one up the barren icy slope as we pull away. It is silent on the bus. Even the students in the back are watching her ascent. Everyone is hoping the same thing—that somewhere they will find someone to welcome them home.

Syr Ruus

The Ice Breakers

Anne Swannell

Excited voices echo in the Douglas firs;
has the lake really formed
a skin between itself
and the new year?
Christmas scarf'd and toque'd,
children test the crystal shore
with tentative boots.
Tossed pebbles prove
how thick truth is.

Skipped stones touch, lift
and touch, skitter
across the glare,
glide into pure distance.

Where the lake enters the woods,
boys dig in their heels,
gouge out frozen pieces, hold them
up to the light,
shouting for the joy of being
here and dangerous
in the unimagined afternoon.

Transported by a miracle
to the glassware department of Birks,
or Eaton's, or The Hudson's Bay,
they are dropping pieces of elegant crystal,
shattering fantastically valuable objects;
transparent plates and delicate goblets,
Soon they are shouldering glittering
chandeliers from the ceiling,
surrounded by mirrors that mirror them fearless
until even they are robbed of their vision.

Now they are climbing a rocky outcrop
overlooking the lake;
they begin to hurl stones, chunks of rock—
the biggest they can lift—
down to the lake's sullen surface.

The lake
creaks on its hinges.

Huge white bubbles
lurch upwards, inch
toward a quaking parallelogram—
a diamond, a triangle—
any rocking window they can get to,
escape—elastic and silent—
into the January air.

The air is colder now,
and bluer where the needles mass.
Toques removed in the heat of attack
are pulled back on,
scarves re-wrapped,

gloves extracted from pockets
for the long trek home.

Exhausted, each rock-hurler
plunks in front of his TV,
activates
the channel changer,
breaks
the ice.

The Ice Breakers

Sarasota

Richard Cumyn

It was still close enough to Christmas for him to feel
the holiday stirring the edge of curtains or pricking
the back of his neck with an errant spruce needle
when he put on his coat. He had never been able to
put aside the holiday with that dug-in, sleeves-rolled-
to-the-elbows kind of determination it took to have
one clear eye on the new year while the lights and
tinsel and baubles returned to their boxes. As usual
he had retreated while Patricia got out her step ladder
to attend to the deed on New Year's Day. Nana
Mouskouri sang two versions of Ave Maria while
Patricia worked. Patricia had a good voice, though
untrained, and she crooned along in accompaniment.
Chafe emerged when it was time to haul the naked
prickly thing out to the curb. He insisted he be the
one to vacuum the needles which were now laid
down in a trail from tree stand to kitchen door. He
made the mess, he would clean it up, he said, as if he
were solely responsible for the death of Christmas.

On Christmas Eve they had driven together after
work to the U-Cut farm near Clayton where she chose
the tree. He told her that she had an artist's eye for
symmetry. They brought it home secured on the roof
of the car with yards of yellow rope which he tied in

intricate knots, the battened conifer conveyed like some newly bagged trophy.

They drank brandy and eggnog while they decorated it. Between them they managed to drop all four of the antique glass baubles Chafe had inherited from his parents, and after the initial shock, began to laugh uncontrollably. They rolled, uproarious on the carpet, over the egg shell pieces of painted glass, hugging their sides and each other. Insisting they replace the smashed ones with home-made decorations, Patricia untangled herself and disappeared into the kitchen. As he waited on the carpet, Chafe squinted to blur the colors of the tree, and the room began to move like an amusement park ride. "This is glorious. This is Christmas," he said, pulling her and the bowl of cold cranberries and warm popcorn she was holding down on top of him.

In the morning they were both sick to their stomachs and afterward returned to bed. Chafe roused first around noon and stole to the basement where he had hidden Patricia's gifts. He took the wrapped presents, which now seemed paltry in light of the amount he had spent on them, and the white plastic bag full of stocking stuff, and went back upstairs. She sat pale on the couch. Beside her on the floor was her underwear still rolled inside her hose, the sheer black pair he had bought her especially for Christmas Eve. The lights of the tree were on. He told her not to look as he filled her stocking. She assured him that turning her head or any other part of her body at that moment was impossible, adding the complaint she raised every year which was that she thought they had agreed not to do Christmas socks anymore. That was something you did as a child or later when you had children of your own, she said.

Chafe ignored her, whistling blithely Good King Wenceslas as he slid bath oil and scented powder, lacy black French underwear, a red and white wooden spinner designed to resemble a hypnotist's aid when it spun, a crossword book, socks, and a glossy woman's magazine into the bulging boot of felt which his mother had sown, stitching "Patricia" in flowing script across the top. Of course then she had to push herself off the couch and fret around the house to find stuffers for him: a handful of unshelled walnuts, a candy cane off a bough, a small wrapped package transferred from under the tree, an unopened bar of soap lifted from the bathroom medicine cabinet.

He pulled each impromptu thing out with delight, exclaiming over it, slowing the process to such a crawl that she became annoyed, threatening to leave him alone there in the middle of the room. But she saw that it meant so much to him. He conjured a mandarin orange from the toe of his stocking and peeled, sectioned, and consumed it before her very eyes. The fruit that he had bought just the day before in the crammed, frantic grocery store was now a wonder in his hands, never before seen by human eyes.

"How can you eat that?" she asked him as the tang of the fruit made her stomach dance.

"It's magic, it's Santa Claus, I'm transformed, I love you," he said.

She said that they had missed a whole side of the tree and he said that it was the most beautiful tree ever. She said that he was becoming tiresome and he said that he could not help it.

"You're not an eight-year-old, Chafe, and I'm not your mother. Everything you do does not delight me."

Then she made her way carefully, queasily, to the laundry room toilet.

* * *

They were hungry by the time his parents arrived for Christmas dinner. As the light faded, the thin colors of the day seemed to coalesce around the table. Patricia had bought

57

Richard Cumyn

tablecloth fabric, a deep wine red with metallic thread tracing a leaf pattern throughout, especially for this meal. Against this molten depth were napkins in gold and red entwined together like the illumination of a medieval book. It had taken her weeks of searching to find the right marriage of colour and texture. Two green candles in plain pewter holders stood in the middle of the table.

His mother gasped when she saw the table. "Chafe, you never told me she was so talented."

Chafe's father said, "Something smells mighty good," which gave Patricia the chance to disappear to tend to the bird.

"I'll help," said Chafe's mother, rising to follow.

"Sit down and have a sherry," said his father. "Give the girl some breathing room."

"You try wrestling a turkey that size all alone, mister. Let me tell you. I know. Twenty-five years of it."

But as Chafe had already gone to help his wife, his mother settled into an armchair, accepting a Dubonnet as consolation. She scanned the tree beside her.

"I don't see the Victorian balls we gave them," she said.

"He can put whatever decorations he wants on his Christmas tree. He's a man now."

"I had so hoped we could get through this without incident," she said.

* * *

Chafe felt his father's monologue coming all through the meal. Patricia was offering seconds of candied yams and mashed potatoes while Chafe stood brandishing the bone-handled carving knife.

"Still plenty of dark meat on this carcass. Dad?"

"Oh, no, I couldn't. I'm still feeling the effects of last week's poker. Did we eat! Hell of a night, Chafe. Your old man cashed out big."

"No kidding, Dad. More wine?" said Chafe as he poured.

"I think I know two things for certain: no matter how much I try to lose, I almost always win; and nothing I win ever satisfies me."

"Which begs my perpetual question, Noah: why continue to play?"

But he ignored his wife's question. "Let me revise my earlier statement: no matter how much I win at poker, I am never satisfied; and I am never really happy unless I am losing."

"I can understand that," said Patricia.

"Oh, then please explain it to me, dear," said Chafe's mother. "This is the one dark corner of masculinity I have never fathomed."

"If you lose, no one resents you."

"Precisely. Clever girl. A very perceptive soul mate you have here, my boy." Patricia blushed but leaned in closer. He had her under his spell. "It's exactly that. When you are down on your luck, you know that your friends are rooting for you in their straight-faced manner. There's no feeling like it. Furthermore, losing implies a change of luck. Therein lies the real source of all joy, you see. The change, that point at which one turns the corner and watches the wheel swing up and the Lady's smile return, that is the sought-after moment. To win endlessly is to lose hope, to tarnish, to begin to feel the others' eyes on your back. But to let a bloke lose it all only to slowly gain it back, well, that's one powerful magnet."

Chafe watched his father's face, which was richly lit by the candlelight, as he talked. More of his life had now been spent living away from this man than with him. His father had

59

constructed a self out of wartime readiness, although he had been too young to fight. His friends, the fast friends, the hard core, were all veterans, accustomed to long stretches away from domesticity. When they came home from combat, many sought the frontiers, the sea or the northern wilderness. This time Noah was in on the action.

"We lived most of the year in bush camps, ate, slept, fought, drank when we could, shot bears that happened to wander in one end of our kitchen tent and out the other. All the while we were mapping a battle plan against the rock for its riches. Gold, silver, nickel, cadmium, uranium. To us, these were words of promise and seduction.

"I tell you a man could become rich just stumbling on a rock as he traversed the wilderness, for surely this was what it was to be a man, out in the air, the vista before him unbroken, spruce and tobacco like a cologne on your skin. There was none of this soul-searching, none of this agonizing over who we were or where we were going. We just were."

Chafe saw a lean, berry-brown young man wearing loose-fitting wool trousers tucked into rubber boots folded over to form a cuff, a heavy leather belt cinching his waist, layers of shirts with button-down pockets holding compass, jeweller's glass, TanToo lotion, cigarettes and matches. In his fist, like an extension of the limb, his father held the handle of an axe at the blade head.

"When it rained we played cards all day and night, under kerosene lamps while the airtight stove blazed and the downpour socked us in. That was the time when a man could go bushed. Bonkers. That was the time he would think about home, about women, hot baths, home cooking, family. It either kept you sane or got you shipped out.

"We used such a word as honour and meant it. Another was trust. A third was love, the love one man can have for another because in that man he sees a reflection of himself. All my life I've tried to recreate that feeling of men together in a wilderness, committed to a single goal, at work, happy, pulled along from day to day by the invisible string of industry.

"I know you've never understood that about me, Margaret. But this young woman, this lovely woman, our son's wife—no, don't look at me that way—she, she can empathize."

"You'd do well to ignore him, Patricia."

"There was no room to be cynical, you see," he said, addressing Patricia but looking straight at Margaret. "No room, no time for such nonsense.

"What we were doing, whether it was looking for gold traces in the clear streams or cutting gridlines or running surveys, was the right thing. We were the yeomen of the good. No one was going to take that away, not from these men who had endured so much. They had fought against Hitler and destroyed him. Now they were returned and no one was going to tell them they had no right to make their way of life, their Democracy, as strong and protected as they could. No one.

"They told me, 'When you get back down there to civilization and your sweetheart, Noah, you think about what you've been fighting for up here. For sure as you're born, you've been fighting as much as the rest of us were over there fighting against the Hun. You've been in a war against complacency and forgetfulness. Kid, by being up here opening up this frontier, mining all the riches this great land of ours has to offer, you've been holding the line against laziness and Communism and ungodliness. Do you understand what we're saying to you? To you we pass the torch. You are the future. My God, Hildebrand, look what's ahead of you. Of all times recorded, this will be the best time to be a man.'"

Chafe's father emptied his wine glass. His eyes were damp.

Richard Cumyn

61

"Do you remember when you and your brothers were growing up, we'd drive north of a Saturday and tramp around the abandoned mines?"

"Yes, I do, Dad."

"You little guys couldn't take the heat."

They had followed their father in the dry heat while flies bit and branches slashed across their faces and their throats felt full of sand. "Nothing like up North, boys," he said to them by way of encouragement. "Look at that," he would exclaim, "schist, magnetite, pyrrhotite." He broke apart hunks of weathered rock with the blunt side of his axe for them to see the inside of the planet, where it all began, and they looked up into his face for some clue because they were unable to see what it was that had so enraptured him. It was as if he could see the rivers of molten rock, the folding, the faulting, syncline and anticline, all held in the clean face of a rock.

At cuts all along the highway he would halt the car and scale half-way up the salmon-colored face with his hammer stuck in his belt. Traffic flashed by as they sat waiting for him. Always, batting distractedly at the veil draped across their eyes, he fought the invisible gauze that blinded them to what it was to be a man in the world. A man carves his signature into the landscape. A man sets a structure against chaos. A man wills, and by doing so changes the very nature of time and space. The boys were hungry and thirsty. The flies bloodied them at the hairline. They did not understand.

His mother broke the reverie. "The only thing I remember about that, Patricia, is Noah calling out the car window, in a voice loud enough to crack glass, 'Where do the men go?' which means," she added for Patricia's benefit, although Chafe could see that his wife understood perfectly what it meant, "where do the men go to drink in this woebegone town? Where is the smoke-filled longhouse, the boat house, the sweat lodge? Where can I go to get away from the wife?"

"You lacked female companionship, Margaret, that is all."

"I lacked a husband."

As she lay in bed that night, Patricia said something that put a cap on the evening. She told Chafe she was afraid that he was going to turn into his father, but also that he would not.

* * *

Chafe bought a bouquet of carnations, pastel interspersed with white ones left over from Christmas, a week after New Year's. On the advice of the florist he kept them in water overnight in the coolest corner of the basement. When he went down to get them in the morning, the whole space was filled with such a bouquet that it seemed the cement walls were draped in a visible perfume. He wanted to keep the flowers himself for their redolence of spring. Instead, he replaced the plastic wrap they had come in, dried the ends of the stems on some paper towelling, attached the card to which he signed both his name and Patricia's, and got into the car. His parents' high-crowned dirt road had not been sanded after the night's ice storm. He kept the car in the middle and prayed that he not meet an oncoming vehicle. An empty white Ford Tempo was nose down in the ditch in front of the Jenkinses, their only neighbours for a kilometer in either direction. Chafe slowed to look and, seeing no one in the car, continued. The approach to the house was on the down slope and he had to be careful to decelerate soon enough and to apply the brakes smoothly to avoid skidding past the entrance to the driveway.

His mother answered the door. "Happy anniversary," he said, offering the flowers. She brought the bouquet to her nose.

Richard Cumyn

She was dressed in a black and white plaid sports jacket, man style over a white blouse clasped at the neck and sleeves in gold, along with trim black slacks, and low-heeled shoes. A suitcase stood just inside the entrance.

"You're going somewhere?"

"Carnations are a very smart choice," she said. "They keep for ages. Let me just put them in water. Can I make you a cup of coffee?"

"I didn't really plan to stay." He followed her into the kitchen where he handed her the packet of preservative that came with the flowers.

"Your father is out on an errand. He shouldn't be too long, I should think, if you want to wait for him."

"Where are you off to?"

"Some people just don't know how to drive in this weather. He's driving a young woman home. Did you see her car on the way in? Why someone would drive a white car in winter is beyond me. The tow truck will scoot on past it, I'm sure. Let me make you a cup of instant, Chafe."

"I've got to be on my way."

"But it would...I think he would be so pleased to see you here when he got back."

"We had made plans for the day."

"You must thank Patricia for the flowers. They're lovely."

"Actually, I picked them out."

"But here is her name on the card, signed by you, quite obviously—I do that all the time myself, signing Noah's name to cards and such, it's so much easier than trying to track him down."

"Will you tell me what's going on?"

"You don't think I meant, 'Thank your wife for picking out the flowers,' do you? I am fully aware of the capabilities of you young husbands nowadays."

"Who is Dad driving home?"

"She reminded me of one of those girls from Personnel. They call it Human Resources now, don't they? You know the type who comes around with the card for so-and-so who is having her baby or getting married or retiring. By the time it gets to you the card is always crammed full with signatures and now, with this pretty and pleasant and efficient person hanging over you, you have to come up with something new to say."

"What will I tell him?"

"How about, 'Best wishes in your new life'? I always liked that one."

"Can't you work it out?"

"The first time it happened I was so angry I screwed my wedding ring off and threw it across the room. I remember it bounced off the fireplace screen and landed in his leather chair where it slid down a crack and lodged under the springs. I felt stronger than I had ever been in my life. I picked that chair up like it was that little rocker of yours and I turned it upside down and shook it. Dust came out and some crayons and finally, after minutes of rage, the ring. I picked it up, slid it back on my finger, but was so exhausted I couldn't right the blasted chair. When he came home he found you and your brothers upstairs watching television and me in a heap on the floor. I shook my marriage back into place, Chafe. I've done it enough times I don't care to count. But," she said with a determined laugh, "I just don't have the arm strength anymore."

As he helped his mother across the slippery driveway to her car, Chafe saw Mr. Jenkins spreading salt by his mailbox. His eldest son and daughter-in-law and two grandsons lived with him and his wife in the darkly wooded compound across the road. The son was going to take over the construction business soon,

Richard Cumyn

leaving the old man to his passion, bird-watching. Jenkins was a counter and cataloguer for the Audubon Society both there and in Florida where he and his wife—fifty-five years come June they would be married—wintered near Sarasota.

Chafe spoke the name of the place aloud. "Sarasota." It felt effervescent in his mouth, carbonated, like "Sarsaparilla," but with more of a pop. He said it again as he waved goodbye to his mother as she backed the car tentatively down the driveway, and again as he flicked the wind chimes over the porch. The sound triggered Patricia's voice.

"I'm afraid you're going to turn into him, but I'm also afraid you're not."

Now he knew what he would say in response. It would be what his father would say.

"You can't have it both ways, Patricia. I can't be Sarasota and Sarsaparilla at the same time. You have to choose one or the other."

The thought pleased him. He tinkled the chimes again, and went back inside to wait for his father to come home.

Sarasota

Molly Goes Christmas Shopping

Anne Swannell

The R/C Hopper's got
a three-position speed-control trigger
non-slip steering wheel, self-centering action, a
rechargeable battery, so she says yes to that for Jerry
and yes to an LCD hand-held electronic ball-game
with two skill-levels and auto-scoring
she knows Ron's gonna love and yes
to Imperial Hypersonic Bullet Racers
which feature ultra-fast and hyper-fast speeds
for Jed and Jupiter, and yes to the WWF Superstar
Wrestling Figures for those nutty nephews of hers
and Yes to Foodfighters for the kids next door
(Private Pizza versus The Taco Terror)
and yes to Sit and Drive for her sister's kids
and yes to the Ghost Busters Pin Ball Game for Robert,
and for Andalie's daughter yes to Baby Shivers
who shakes when she's undressed.

She says yes to newborn Pound Puppies made by Irwin
and yes to the Super Brite Micro Mini Cars
with working head and tail lights (though she
almost settled for Tonka's Ramblin' Scramblers)
and yes to the Cobra MISS 11 combat vehicle
which takes care of Max and Mandy nicely and yes

67

and yes to three Teenage Mutant Ninja Turtles
who fight almost as hard as they party
(and do both in a Turtles Party Wagon
which converts to battle-ready
assault vehicle, bombs included),
yes to My Little Pony complete with comb
which Jeanie's always wanting and yes
to a Precious Places Village
with Extra-Precious Accessories for Virginia
and yes and yes and yes oh yes it will
be on her Masterchurge.

Molly Goes Christmas Shopping

Playing Marley's Ghost

Timothy J. Anderson

I t's a silly way to make a living, climbing up an eight foot slide and whooshing out of a chimney in a clatter of chains and a cloud of smoke. But playing Jacob Marley's ghost in *A Christmas Carol* only happens at one time of year, and the entrance is spectacular enough that the audience thinks you are actually doing something when all it really takes is the willingness to climb the ladder and sit down. Do this eight times a week for a month, and then buy Christmas presents with the money you make.

Actors working at Christmas may feel a touch of humbuggery. December brings with it memories of numbingly awful Sunday School pageants and shadowplays, years of playing mute shepherds in striped terrycloth robes and the pain of knowing that once again you have not been asked to play the virgin or the angel, which are the best parts because they have the most to say. Christmas to the professional means earnest characters, changes of heart, and peace on earth eight times a week.

Playing Marley's ghost is no exception. The repentant wraith haunts the skinflint Scrooge on Christmas Eve, wailing his warning to his scoffing former partner, rattling his chains and suffering the torments of the damned. Good moral stuff, Marley, but working at Christmas means less time for browsing through the merchandise piled as thickly and haphazardly as the snow on Winnipeg thoroughfares.

I have ventured into the urban prairie November between shows and quickly lost heart, taking refuge in the overwarm tunnels-in-space which we call pedways or skywalks or Plus 15. By following these tunnels I can reach the major downtown shops without ever setting foot on slushy sidewalks, without fearing my nose will freeze and crack. It takes extra time to follow this labyrinth back and forth through stores and over streets and under squares, but the tinned music drives me through nicely.

My head is full of Christmas songs, not carols but those jangly jingly tunes like "Jingle Bell Rock" which the shopping malls play because they sell more stocking stuffers than "Silent Night" and they manage not to offend anyone who has left the Christian path and wants to shop without feeling pressured into a sentimental religious stupor. The incessant jingling only antagonizes people who dislike popular culture or bad music, or who don't like having their religious festivals coopted by commerce, but they are free to grump "Bah, humbug!" and shop by mail order from the comfort of their homes.

The stores have mounted a good campaign this year, and early shoppers clog the exposed pedway arteries between buildings. They haven't yet discovered they've left someone important off their shopping list, or remembered that Uncle Fred has a birthday December 23rd and someone else is bound to give him the Elvis collector plate they bought on sale at the discount store two blocks away from the warmth of the tunnels. They haven't received their charge card bills, they haven't started worrying about the hard-to-buy-for children who have everything under

$60 already. The skies have graced their expedition with the first real snowfall of the season, and all is merry and bright.

The sleigh bells shimmer away the minutes left of my between-show break, and I weave my way through the slower traffic, barely containing my impatience at the lumbering mass of shoppers who clearly believe everyone should join them in their slow graze under the plastic Christmas boughs.

At one point between stores, suspended over the main street, the crowd reaches a density which suggests a major sale of postal savings Christmas cards, or perhaps a free wrapping station. No-one is moving, except to see past the people in front of them, and I can see people watching from the other direction.

Clinging to the brushed chrome pipe railing in the pedway is a man in dirty and unfashionable denims, with a grimy coat and matted reddish hair. He has a dark beard and dirty hands, knuckle-white from holding on. This is not Santa Claus. Two portly security guards in maroon jackets are trying to pry him loose from the railing. No words are spoken, but the guards are grunting with the effort. The crowd is chattering away, like the sparrows in the trees at Queen's Park. They are watching the spectacle with the sort of detached enjoyment they would bring to a Whoopi Goldberg video. Beyond the crowd I can see more security guards running, and when I turn around I see more coming from that direction too. A half dozen maroon jackets converging on this one man, clinging to the railing in the vague belief that if he can hold on long enough everyone will go away.

The crowd makes passage difficult, but I am determined to get past, refusing to swell the ranks. The man keeps his head down, not meeting the eyes of the dozens of spectators. The guards heave, and for a moment he loses his grip, but his adrenalin is pumping and he manages to lunge for the pipe again,

Timothy J. Anderson

and hangs on with renewed desperation. The crowd becomes more attentive, watching and muttering softly, Christmas packages in their hands.

He raises his head, but he isn't looking at anyone. His eyes are closed. He opens his mouth and I notice his teeth are rotten. His face is red from the strain of holding on. He bellows, perhaps to the guards but it seems more like a cry to the universe, "BUT I HAVE NO MONEY."

The voice comes straight from the core of his being. It is the fully connected voice I work towards as an actor. It is the cry of torment which I can only approximate as the ghost of Jacob Marley. It stops me momentarily, long enough to witness what happens next.

They laugh. All those people, with their Christmas lists and their charge cards and their warm clean clothes, they laugh outright. Not a nervous titter, but a cruel and open laugh. Dozens of ordinary people. There's a woman in her mid-thirties wearing a sheer long-sleeved blouse and immaculate grey flannels and black pumps and she's with another woman in a light blue coat, and they are pointing and laughing.

One of the maroon-jacketed guards says "Neither do I, buddy," and the crowd laughs again.

I keep moving, my brain stuck between gears and pushing me along, vaguely registering "Holly Jolly Christmas" and telling me I am not contributing to this spectacle. I have a brief fantasy about standing in front of that man, shielding him from the laughter, and berating the mob for their lack of compassion, their willingness to humiliate someone who is powerless. I keep walking through the skywalks along my accustomed route to the theatre.

As I sit in front of my dressing room mirror, getting ready to climb that ladder and come whooshing out of the chimney for

the second performance, I am suddenly crying. I have been poor. I have been hungry. When you have nothing you don't decide to steal; you make a daily decision not to steal. And there comes a day when you are too defeated and tired and weak to make that decision any more.

A keen awareness of my failure to speak for him haunts me. I wipe my eyes, repair my makeup, don the chains and lockboxes with which Marley's ghost is burdened, and climb the ladder to the top of the slide. In the bluish light of the wings I prepare myself for the big entrance. The bells ring, the smoke snakes out the fireplace, and gravity pushes me down and into the bright light of the stage.

When I rise from Scrooge's hearth and hear the audience laugh at Marley's desperate and decaying ghost, my knuckles go white and my warning to the complacent rips out of me, tearing through my throat, giving voice to the pain born of countless unthinking cruelties. The laughter stops. They are hearing his voice, his desperation, and in the make-believe world of the theatre it becomes more real to them than the wheedling beggars and unheralded destitutes of the streets outside. I no longer think this is a silly way to make a living.

When the curtain falls and the applause swells I am thinking of him and the gift he has unknowingly given to me. My eyes are wet with gratitude and the unspoken thoughts lumped in my throat: I have not completely failed you, they have been silenced, you have been heard, you have been heard, you have been heard...

73

Timothy J. Anderson

Traverse Afar

Alice Major

*Snowfall quiet as
candle light. Cold air
near the window
moves like perfume
toward the room's
warm center and
brings the honey-
slippered scent of
freesia, five flowers
from another
season, an other-
oriented place.*

*All the industry that brings these yellow blossoms
here. The aero-whine of metal wings, the wheeled
clattery of shopping malls, the christmas-induced
cameraderie, greetings punched out like staples
with your sales receipt, carols lifting off like
aircraft over the buyers' heads.*

*Now calm brought
face to face with
calm—a careful
seam, ragged edges
folded out of
sight. The suture
invisible in
this slow air, this
incense composed
of spring and still
snow. In the bleak
midwinter, this
reverent gift.*

The Second Coming of Internet

Dianne Linden

Ever since the Wisepersons brought gold and frankincense and myrrh to the infant Jesus, gift-giving has been an important part of celebrating Christmas. It's been a tricky part for some of us, however, so that should guarantee welcome for a new and improved arrival on the shopping horizon. I'm referring, of course, to the coming, for a second, successful season, of Holiday Internet.

There need be no more scuttling past the Salvation Army Santa Claus this Christmas as we exit our neighbourhood liquor store, eyes downcast, arms filled with bottles of brandy and rum and single-malt Scotch. No more last-minute mall searches for modest gifts we can tart up with wrapping paper and the right card. (Let's say a recent acquaintance phones on the twenty-first and hints darkly that she'd like to drop by with a gift. "It's nothing much, really," she says, and we long to take her at her word. Give her a loaf of banana bread wrapped in Saran Wrap in return. But there's a chance she might appear at our door with a $30.00 basket of balms, scents and lotions from the Body Shop. In her Christmas shopping vocabulary that may not actually be much. But it's more than banana bread. We didn't even use a recipe. And we feel we have to be prepared.)

Holiday Internet will be like an early-arriving, electronic Santa Claus for people who work at the only jobs currently available in Alberta: those involving tasks formerly carried out by a minimum of two other people. There is a fee attached to Internet membership, of course, and shoppers will pay for what they buy but (and here is the amazing part of the enterprise) with electronic currency. Not with money. The fact that this new currency does not actually exist, we're told, is not a matter for concern. Buyer and seller both regarding its existence as real will apparently make it so. It's a loaves and fishes kind of thing which Jesus might actually be more comfortable with than many Canadian consumers. Not that it matters. Jesus isn't really the focus of Christmas anymore.

It's not surprising. Time has passed. Values have shifted. Even if we sleep a lot, we have to be aware that the world of the nineties and the world of that first Christmas have very different characteristics. To start with, there are more people now than there were then. We love to invent gadgets to do our work and solve our problems so, therefore, there are also more microwave ovens, fax machines, remote control television sets; more incandescent light bulbs, hockey skates, Japanese noodles, freeze-dried strawberries, hiking equipment, high-speed modems, cordless telephones and designer label clothing. The richness of our world in terms of retail outlets, bar codes, laser beams and money-back guarantees is more than most of us can comprehend. It's a fact that more gifts were returned on Boxing Day last year in Edmonton, than Christians sacrificed to lions on an average afternoon in the Roman Empire.

Objectively put, the world has become lowmyth, and Holiday Internet fits in with the mentality of the times. The problem is that, in many ways, Christmas and those of us who try to take it mytho-seriously do not. We're presented with problems we find difficult to resolve. Science teaches us, for example, that the virgin birth is an unlikely means of reproduction. Shepherds wandering off from reliable jobs because of something said by an angel offend our 1990's high-unemployment-rate sensibilities. And modern astronomers have yet to document a single incident in which a star increased in intensity and travelled outside its orbit, although that's what we're told happened, in order for the Wisepersons to find Bethlehem.

In defense of Christmas Story-Thinking, the Wisepersons did spend a lot of time up on their ziggurats, making a close study of the stars. They watched the sky as faithfully as we watch television and our computer screens, so their relationship to heaven was obviously more intense than ours.

When I observe that the sky is higher than it used to be, I know I'm not the first person to advance the theory. Unlike the people who built the Tower of Babel, modern Europeans and North Americans travel to the tops of mountain-high buildings every day and don't come down speaking different languages. A few Conservatives in Ottawa actually did spend the night at the top of the Toronto Space Needle hoping to improve their French, although it didn't work. And last summer a young man from Saskatoon named Michael Icarus flew his Piper Cub directly into the sun until he ran out of fuel, but he never got close enough for the wax holding on the wings of his plane to melt.

It may well be that if we asked shoppers a week before December 24th whether using Holiday Internet would have simplified their lives, the majority would answer yes. I, however, still feel that the way the Wisepersons got ready for that First Christmas is the best preparation: going outside, looking up at the night sky.

Dianne Linden

Most of the set-pieces from the original event are still there.

The moon, for instance, continues her monthly wax and wane. Her periods are as reliable as clockwork. Every clear night in the history of human life on this planet she's shown us at least a sliver of her patient, pock-marked face. And the stars are there as well. Orion. Ursa Major. Cassiopeia. The Pleiades. They've seen all kinds of networks come and go—some concerned with much more dangerous matters than shopping, and it hasn't altered the basic rhythm of their lives in any way.

As often as I can during this Christmas season, I'm going to set up my Amateur Stargazer's Telescope on the back steps of my house and focus on some pin-point of light that is mythologically related to the Star of Bethlehem. I'll think about my royal predecessors, speaking to the stars in a long-forgotten language. ("Greetings. I'm Balthazar. Are you...Sirius?") And I'll feel centered. More resourceful. Committed to the welfare of my fellowpersons but, like the stars, not overly involved. I'll be thinking about it this way: The world is not hurtling toward perfection as rapidly as I'd hoped it would be. And heaven is farther away than it once was. That may all be for the best. It leaves room for hope. It leaves room, above the networking of electronic shop-and-chat lines, for the continued existence of a Very Significant Story.

The Ram

Jannie Edwards

It's Christmas Eve and I know you are dying
on the coast, without me to witness.
I have listened to your laboured breathing on the phone,
each breath a ragged revolt against death.
I have chosen to be here, with the family I have made,
skating on my friend's pond, while the quick children
weave, their cries feasting on the night's clarity
and the intoxication of morning, the best morning of the year.

My father. The Ram. Solid as earth.
How many times have you squared off against death
with your devotion to life, your doctor's husbandry,
your healing horns. When I saw you last,
you were turning into a bird: bright bird eyes,
skin stretched over hollow bones.
How small do you have to get before you can fly away
from these spare bones, this bleached life.

Tonight I must locate you in a constellation—The Ram—
the way I have sited my mother in Great Bear.
It is not easy to locate your sky grave.
It is not easy to imagine you flying alone.
It is not easy to make light of my love.

Christmas Eve in Thumbprint

Marie Anne McLean

J oe Lansbury didn't like driving cab, and he didn't like working Christmas Eve but he didn't really have much choice.

Joe had been hitting the bottle for about five years when he went on a really big bender and lost his job at the fertilizer plant. Myrna said to him that she had just about had enough. Either Joe quit or she would leave him.

Joe knew that he needed Myrna more than he needed the booze so he joined AA. When he had been dry for about six months his brother-in-law Milt Starsky offered him a job. Milt seemed to have more faith in Joe than Joe did.

Thumbprint hadn't had a taxi service since Fred Melic, the owner of the cab, had run off with the owner of the Klip'n'Kurl. Milt offered to set up a new company with two Plymouth K-cars from the Chrysler dealership if Joe would be the president of the company.

As the head of the company, Joe really felt that he couldn't ask Willard Marchenko, his only employee, to work Christmas Eve so there he was. He had read the entire first aid manual, and was settling down to play solitaire when the phone rang at about ten-thirty.

It was Marie Smollett and she was crying.

Marie lived with her pain of a mother on a scruffy farm halfway between Thumbprint and Weed Creek. It had always seemed to Joe that Mattie Smollett only gave Marie house room so that she would have someone to pick on.

"Joe, can you come and get me? She's in a real temper and she threw me out. I can go to my Aunt Evelyn's if you come and get me. I don't have any other way to get out of here and she means it. Please Joe. I hate to call you out on Christmas Eve..." Marie's voice trailed off into silence.

About the only thing worse than working on Christmas Eve would be to have to take a run out on the road to Weed Creek. It seemed that the Saskatchewan Department of Highways had entirely forgotten that road. It still had frost-boils from last spring. Even more discouraging was the thought of facing Big Mattie Smollett when she was in a temper. Big Mattie was a mean drunk.

"Sure I'll come Marie. It will take me about a half an hour or so. Just you sit tight."

"I'll wait for you out at the main road Joe. The driveway here is real hard to turn around in." Marie paused, "And thanks Joe..."

Joe didn't take very long to get ready for the trip. Outside he looked up to the night sky. The clouds had been crowding in lower all afternoon making the sky that dangerous kind of gray that reminds you that the weather is the enemy. It was definitely blizzard weather. That didn't bother Joe. He had grown up in Saskatchewan and he knew that the weather was capricious and dangerous. He had a good blizzard kit in the trunk of the cab and he knew the road well.

The trip out to Mattie's farm only took a little more than the usual half-hour or so. Joe knew that the trip back to town was going to take a long time because the wind had arrived and it was serious about reminding people that they were mortal. The snow was driving in sideways like it wanted to stab somebody.

Joe didn't worry much when Marie wasn't at the turnoff to meet him. It was too cold to be standing out there in the wind. Joe turned in at the farm and drove down the narrow lane to the yard.

He arrived in front of the house in time to see a slow kind of tug-of-war on the front step. Big Mattie was standing on the top step screaming and pulling on the handle of a large suitcase. Marie was standing on the bottom step pulling it feebly with both hands. Just as Joe got out of the cab, Mattie shoved the case and let go. Her daughter fell and the suitcase fell on top of her.

It was right about then that Joe realized that Marie was about eight months pregnant. He had probably seen her recently but not registered the fact of her condition. Myrna was always saying that Joe was not a noticing kind of fellow.

Joe stooped to help Marie up and put his arm around her to lead her into the back seat. He got a blanket from the trunk and tucked it around her. Mattie scowled and backed away into the house.

Joe turned the cab and headed back to town. The road was nearly obscured by the wind and snow. Joe drove slowly and concentrated on the road. He didn't try to talk to Marie. It seemed to him that she would probably like a little privacy right now. He could hear her quietly crying.

About a mile down the road, Marie gave a low moan and then she spoke. "Joe, I think my water just broke!"

"Not in my cab! No, Marie, this is your first baby, you get all kind of false alarms with your first. Why when Myrna had Big Donnie, our oldest, she was having false labour and pains and

Christmas Eve in Thumbprint

stuff for a whole month before he finally was born."

"Joe, I don't think this is a false alarm." Marie's voice held a hint of hysteria.

"Well, I'll turn around real careful and we can go back to the house."

"NO!" Marie shouted. "I'll have it in the yard before I'll go have my baby in that house with her."

"Okay, okay I won't do it, I'll keep heading for town. We probably got a lot of time. You know when Myrna had Big Donnie, she was in labour for about thirty-six hours." Joe realized that this was probably not the right thing to say to someone who was about to have her first baby. "Just relax, Marie, I know what to do. I'll call Myrna on the CB."

Myrna always listened to the CB when Joe worked nights. It kept her company, and she liked to keep up on the "news." Myrna would be there and she would have advice for sure. Myrna was an advising kind of woman.

Myrna was there just like he knew she would be and she knew what to do.

She would call the hospital first and then Dr. Cameron, the new young one who didn't make a fuss over night calls. She said she would let Constable Tully know, and Dieter Smale over at Thumbprint Ambulance Service. Then if it looked like Joe needed help there would be someone to provide it. Myrna was good at crises.

Joe reassured Marie and kept on driving. Marie's moans were getting closer together but Joe knew he could make it. He wasn't ready to have anybody born in his cab.

As they approached the edge of town the moans seemed to be longer and the breaks between them seemed to be shorter. The cab came to the long curve by Starsky's Chrysler Dealership, and Joe could see that the wind had let up a bit and the road was clearer.

Marie Anne McLean

He accelerated just a touch and that was about when he seemed to use up his luck because the tires hit a patch of black ice. The cab went into a long slow slide toward the ditch. It slid gracefully through the snow ridge from the government snowplough and stopped directly under the giant neon five-point Chrysler insignia that marked the entrance to Starsky Motors.

Marie cried out in fear.

Joe called Myrna to tell her what had happened. His voice cracked as he choked back the rising panic.

Myrna was in the middle of reassuring Joe when Marie yelled "It's coming now! It's coming right now Joe! Oh God!"

Right then Joe went all calm inside. "It's okay Marie, I'm here. I can do this. Why I just read the manual tonight!" While he was speaking, Joe was climbing out of the driver's seat and into the back beside Marie.

And there in the back of his cab he helped Marie deliver her boy. He took off the reversible down-filled orange vest that Myrna had bought at the Saan Store for his birthday. It was warm from his body as he wrapped it around the new baby. Then he put the baby onto Marie's abdomen just like the manual said and Marie curled her arms around her son.

Joe was filled with awe. He reached out and curved his big hand around the wet dark little head. "Jesus Christ."

Marie was laughing and crying. She looked out the back window of the cab as the ambulance and the police car pulled up onto the shoulder of the road. Constable Tully, Doctor Cameron and Dieter Smale were climbing down into the ditch carrying the packages and bags they needed to help her.

Marie looked down at her son. Then softly and solemnly she spoke. "Yeah Joe, and here come the three wise men!"

Christmas at the Bissell Centre

Gale Sidonie Sobat

8:30 am

patrons arrive
doors are open
clientele spills in
business day begins
business as usual
the business of staying alive
another day
and then another cold night

the clerks smiling
hand out complimentary coffee
and Christmas cheer
greet the regular customers
the ragman, the hawker, the huckster
the knights of the road
the ladies of the night
this morning they flood the market
and the clerks smiling hope there is enough
food in the larders for turkey dinner

10:30 am

by mid-morning they are seated together
smoking roll-your-owns
leaning back in rickety chairs
like so many boardroom executives
around a table
at the old boys' club

you'll recognize them
captains of industry
the entrepreneur, the business magnate
the tradesman, the trafficker, the tycoon
the newsdealer, the liquor merchant
assets liquidated
they're here for the closing-out sale

11:00 am

at the Bissell bazaar
it's a mass market
the shoppers peruse the aisles
malinger in the haberdashery
drape tired furs over tired limbs
slip slightly used footwear
over feet swollen with travel-wear
sigh and assess and select
take stock of the sundries
take note of the billboard
just across the street:
"Christmas begins at Eaton's Centre"

Christmas at Bissell

Noon: the Christmas Luncheon

the line forms on the street
moving slowly, incessantly
the people of the inner city
with no purchasing power
wait patiently for a plate

and listen to the shrill voices of the young choir
  brought in from suburban privilege
  to sing a carol or two
  for the urban market
applaud politely
request "Silent Night"

the ticket agent takes their tickets
they thank him politely
some embrace him
wish him Merry Christmas
and though they may be reeling
from any drug on the market
or smelling of stale wine and tobacco
he returns their offer
gives the asking price

in two hours
the very young
the very old
and those lost somewhere in between
are a little less hungry
they go out into the Christmas air
with a gift of toiletries from Santa
as I run off to my last-minute shopping

87

Gale Sidonie Sobat

tonight on Christmas Eve
where will they be
these patrons of the street
come-on men
personnel of urban squalor?
canvassing or soliciting
cooped-up in one-room solitude
roaming the sidewalks for the highest bidder
singing a song of the season to an empty bottle
against a backdrop of impervious skyscrapers
consumers of the inner city
are slouching towards Bethlehem

Christmas at Bissell

Living Colour

Adele Megann

C olleen is lying on the living room chesterfield, a cushion over her head. Her parents are in the kitchen, her brothers and sisters are somewhere in the house. The corduroy skirt she wore to Mass this morning clutches at her buttocks, thighs, calves. The brown skirt is a gift from Santa, who shops at her mother's favourite store. Apparently.

grease
your sisters every year where is my have to
cat tugs at tree
again? why do we not that one I said no
thick smell of goose edges to burn
that girl's attitude put that
rattle dry branches aluminum ornaments
my sisters that down expecting us
harpsichord music father's favourite thin tinny
not this year
again and again tin tin tin
lazy I'll baste it
goose still dry
I'll tired her
and greasy
attitude

8-track repeats automatically
around and around
I have give it back have a to your
brother headache I it's not his
cat eating tinsel
by myself not his
Program 4 Program 1
goose grease stuffs mouth throat nostrils eyes
UN-GRATE-FUL GIRL
he'll choke

From beneath the cushion, Colleen peeks out at the racket. The cat gives a low branch one last tug and flies off. The tree comes to rest against its guy wires, shuddering. Displayed under the tree, surrounded by the still-wrapped presents (they do that part after dinner) is the crèche. Just like every crèche Colleen has ever seen. Mary is wearing a blue robe with a white veil, Joseph is enrobed in purple, and the new-born baby Jesus has thick, wavy blonde hair.

Colleen is about to duck back under the cushion, when through the haze of goose smoke (good thing they don't have a smoke detector), she spies a stirring under the tree. The ceramic Mary begins to swell, she overflows the wooden stable, bloating up like an air mattress, until she teeters above the living room floor (like one of those balloon clowns weighted at the bottom that they used to punch), larger than life, seven feet maybe. Her hands are still held together prayerfully as they were when she knelt before her just-born child. "Jeepers. I'm a visionary," thinks Colleen, "Do I have to report this to Father O'Brien?"

> bishops nodding gravely in thick red parlours
> my toe deep in carpet
> theologians are investigating
> *what was our lady's message*
> people tramping mud grass dry leaves
>   on our living room floor
> AWE-THEN-TIC
> strangers selling plastic rosaries on our sidewalk
> becoming a nun have to now then
>   a saint forever a saint
> movies about me when I'm dead and canonized
> PICK someone else
> I was never asked...

"... if I wanted to wear blue."

"Excuse me?"

"I was never asked if I wanted to wear blue," repeated Mary. Colleen has to assume that she hears Mary's voice, because the lips don't move. "Blue doesn't look so good on me. If we could have afforded nice clothes back then, I would have chosen yellow, a gold yellow to stroke my brown skin, to vibrate with the warmth of my skin, the earth, sun."

"Brown skin?" An alabaster white is what Colleen sees, the still lips a 40's-movie-star red, eyes blue as a blonde's can be, the cheeks a modest blush, the forehead solid. Not brown, thinks Colleen, but not like anyone she's ever known to live in St. John's, either.

Adele Megann

"I'm not an English schoolgirl, you know. I am a Semite, Middle Eastern. You've heard those words somewhere before, haven't you..."

Lebanese girls at school
if that tree falls over
they laugh with big white teeth and long black hair
thick and straight
go to mass like us
if that cat's eating tinsel
Joanne in the Top 5 of best friends
born here parents born there never
talk about Lebanon
once Joanne brings crumbly sweet candy to school
if that cat chokes
haval? hovel? holiv?
shocks the teeth with sweetness
it's a Lebanese tradition she said
oh!
only once
they have Newfoundland accents
lazy girl on the chesterfield
Michelle Donna Susan
names like us
I'll choke her
talk like us

"Like Joanne. Do you look like Joanne?" Joanne, unlike Colleen, looks great in yellow.
"I've never met Joanne. Maybe." Mary still appears white and blonde, but as Colleen stares into the cheap

ceramic that masks Mary's face, she notices in the
black opening between the lips a spark of movement,
a yawning shadow. Darkness surrounds, draws
Colleen into the glow of invisible teeth she knows are
there. Stop, she thinks, not so fast, and I don't like
wearing brown so much myself so there and . . .

tree shakes
a tinsel dance shoots about the room
blue green red yellow flashes
branches dip and bow jostle of tin balls
needles stand up they sing those needles
a song of hums a harmony
a two thousand part harmony
shepherd flourishes hooked staff
how did he get barefoot
king losing his crown
dance
Mrs. Claus yanks pins from her hair
wise men drink wassail with the little match girl
get back on your branch
robes uncovering a frenzy of cloth
frosty the snowman is melting
angels throw pine cones at the nutcracker prince
mary didn't just say eyem outta here
no way
did she?

Adele Megann

The Stepfather's Story

Shirley A. Serviss

I wasn't the first man
to marry a woman carrying another's child.
Nor the last. Even in good Jewish families
like mine. Who would have to know?
I thought it would be our secret.
Do you think the angels could keep
their mouths shut? Announcing his birth
to the shepherds: Christ the Lord!

And then the wise men showed up
and the cat was really out of the bag.
Mind you, so was the gold, incense and myrrh
and I have to admit the money came in handy
when we had to flee to Egypt.
Just compensation I figure.
If they hadn't told Herod, we could have
gone back to Nazareth where I had a good
name as a carpenter.

You think it's easy living
in a blended family? Especially in these
shared custody situations
when the other parent wants a voice
in the decisions. And He'd never talk
directly to me. Always sending angels

94

with messages—directives from on high.
It's lucky I can read
the writing on the wall.

It's tough being a stepfather
especially when the boy's real Dad
is the Almighty
authority on everything.
I make furniture, build houses.
God made heaven and earth,
and do you think He'd let me forget it?

I tried to be easy on the boy—
give him a break. A stepfather can afford
to be a bit indulgent. It's no reflection on me
how the kid turns out. His real Father
was a bit hidebound, I thought—
all those "thou shalts" and "shalt nots."
But Jesus had a self-righteous streak
in him too. "That's not how things are done
in my Father's house," he'd say,
as if I gave a carpenter's damn.

I taught him everything I knew—
how to mortise a corner, drive a nail,
measure everything twice.
A guy needs to earn an honest living,
but you just can't fight heredity.
He had this fascination for sleight of hand:
calming the waves, turning water into wine,
rousting evil spirits—you know the kind of thing
I mean. No money in it, but he built up
quite a following. Just like his real Father.
I warned him he'd come to no good end,
but do you think he'd listen to me,

what with his Father calling him all the time?
I don't have to tell you he broke his mother's heart.
He always was Mary's favourite—
firstborn son and all.

As for me, maybe it's just natural
to love your own flesh
and blood more—even though I tried
my level best to be fair.
But it was always "Joseph"
this, and "Joseph" that. I wished
the kid would sometimes call me "Dad."

The Stepfather's Story

The Midwife's
Tale

Mary Woodbury

Strange events have been happening in our family. First, Cousin Elizabeth discovered she was with child. We all felt sorry for her because she had no children. Her husband Zechariah was struck dumb for doubting the news of her pregnancy. The old guy didn't speak for months. Elizabeth, bless her heart, has not minded the silence as he's one of those husbands with strong opinions and a sharp tongue. Let's hope Zechariah's son doesn't take after him.

Shock number two came closer to home. My daughter Mary, the one with lovely eyes, came to me anxious as a cat, four months before her marriage to Joseph, the carpenter here in Nazareth. I was sewing fancy trimming onto her bridal nightdress when she whispered low, "Momma, I've had the strangest dream." I put the stitching down to listen. She's always been introspective. I'm a plain spoken woman myself. Her home will be more tranquil than mine.

"I dreamt a handsome young man in white robes came into my room. He said, 'Peace and blessing from the God of Abraham and Sarah.'"

I understood my daughter's fear and touched her arm to gentle her. Messengers from Elohim are rare and bring mixed blessings.

I thought about calling the midwife Hulda and the old prophetess to help me interpret the young girl's dream. But Mary hurried on.

"Momma, he saw my agitation and comforted me. 'God is good. You have been chosen to bear the future king of Israel. You are pregnant with a child of nobler lines than good king David. Call him Jesus. He'll be a great human being, so close to God he will be called son.'"

"'Impossible,'" I said, 'Joseph and I haven't ...'"

(Mind you, old woman that I am, I suspect they've come close, for they are young and full of ardour.)

"He interrupted me and said, 'The spirit and the power of God are with you, Mary. The child is holy, like your cousin Elizabeth's, only more so. Her child will be a prophet. Yours will be a son of God.'" Mary paused.

"What did you say to that?" I asked.

"I was so shocked, mother, I couldn't think of any great response. 'All right, Gabriel,' I said. 'What can I say? I serve God.' Then he left. So, Momma, what do I do now?"

I fetched Hulda and the holy woman. They brought other village women with them. I made tea. The day was warm and clear. The men were in the fields. We left them to it as this was women's business.

The old prophetess spoke first.

"Anna, my dear, your family has been chosen for special roles. Elohim has recognized your worth. Too often glory has gone to the powerful, grace has imbued the rich. History has been carried by warriors. Finally the spirit that breathes through the universe has selected two humble women to set the stage for a cosmic drama. Bearing, birthing, living, loving, dying—the cycle continues."

The Midwife's Tale

Hulda addressed Mary. "Are you sure Joseph and you didn't get carried away?"

Mary blushed. I spoke for her. "We have kept a canny eye on them. If Elohim has made her pregnant, what will we tell Joseph?"

"He'll probably believe it is his anyway. Shorten the engagement," Hulda said.

The prophetess spoke. "Perhaps they slipped up, perhaps they didn't. We'll discover later when the child grows up if he is from God or not. What if it's a girl? Do we throw it back in the face of Elohim? Our people will not listen to a woman prophet for long." I heard bitterness in her tone. The rest of what she suggested made sense.

"Send her away to visit relatives. If Elizabeth is with child, send Mary to help. Bring her home in time to marry Joseph." The wise woman dipped her crust in tea.

All eyes turned to me. I motioned to Mary. Her face was pale with worry. "Go fetch your bundle and your cloak," I said. She lowered her head and left the parlor.

We women prayed for her and her unborn child.

"It is better than a curse," said one woman kindly.

"What ever will the men say?" asked another.

"They'll make it their story or sweep it under the mat," said Hulda stoically.

We sighed. As each woman left she embraced me and wished us well. I arranged with Hulda to be available as the time was complete. With a slip of a girl like Mary, such a dreamer, she'll forget all skill when labour starts.

Mary cried as we parted. A mother and daughter should be together during those expectant days. I felt better when Elizabeth sent word.

99

Mary Woodbury

"Cousin Anna, your girl arrived," her messenger reported. "What a gentle creature. You have done a fine job raising her. She, like you, has a stubborn streak that will keep her steadfast. And yet, she is a singer, sitting dreamy by the window, watching for Joseph or praising God. She could grow into a holy woman.

"Mark my words, when she first approached my door, the babe within leapt in untimely joy. Is it an omen? Zechariah continues mute. What a laugh. The old man writes me notes if he wants more dates or mash. I'll send Mary back before Hulda comes to deliver me. Where would our race be without midwives, I ask you?" Thus ended her message.

The three months dragged by in spite of all the work the mother of the bride must do—the seams to sew, the towels to hem, the potter to haggle with. You know what it's like.

When Mary returned, her cheeks were glowing, her eyes misty. "I have missed you, Momma, but Elohim drew near. Surely the spirit is in everyone, waiting to be recognized. I am one of many sisters who will bring forth hope and love."

Hearing that, I knew the girl was getting too mystical. So I set her to culling beans, while I arranged the wedding party.

Joseph and Mary married and moved to his house. The wedding feast was smaller than I originally planned, but then mothers rarely get their way. As for the early arrival of a child, most villagers will forgive, imagining the usual. Should we call this child "love without interruption?" Not bad for the name of the offspring of Elohim— but then I've always been an earthy woman. Mary says they'll call him Jesus, like the dream commanded. Jesus—love without interruption. What difference does it make—the child is God's.

Speaking of babies, Elizabeth had a bouncing baby boy. The rabbi and the village gathered for the circumcision and the

The Midwife's Tale

naming. They chanted, "Name him Zechariah after the papa." But the old boy wrote on his tablet, "His name is John." When the crowd agreed, Zechariah opened up his mouth and praised God. He's been talking non-stop ever since.

Pity poor Elizabeth, she'll die content because she's borne a son—but if John is a prophet like Zechariah claims, he will die young. We Hebrews kill our prophets. Most races do.

When the cold winds blew from the north, the Roman bureaucrats declared a census. Everyone must travel back to their home town. That means Joseph, too. He is of Bethlehem, so he and Mary need to journey all the way from Nazareth to pay taxes and make their mark. What foolishness.

Thank goodness we provided a donkey as part of her dowry. She is exhausted and it can carry her. I wish I could have gone but Hulda has promised to visit her sister, the midwife of Bethlehem, in case my daughter's time arrives. Mary is convinced this child is special. I felt the same about her. Don't all mothers think of their children as marked by God?

She is so young and Joseph so earnest. I worried as I kissed them both goodbye. Will a man like that, so secretive, so silent, be good company for my open-hearted Mary? He has a good trade. But he's a brooder. Not much fun after forty, if you hear what I'm saying. I hope she has daughters to talk to. If this firstborn is a prophet or a king, he won't be much solace to his mother. Oh well, leave it be, Anna old woman, you'll be dead and gone before that drama unfolds.

I gave her an extra hug, so close I felt the child move in her womb. I pressed into her hands a bundle of soft cloths that I hemmed myself in tiny stitches. The fabric in my fingers reminded me of my own journey to birthing. Magical moments shot through with pain and wonder. Now I'm sounding sentimental like my daughter. Excuse me while I dry my eyes.

101

Mary Woodbury

Hulda hurried home with the news of Jesus' birth. The village women gathered in my room again, to hear how it went with Mary. The men as usual were in the fields or shooting dice. Births don't interest them unless the issue is theirs.

"The village was awash with returning relatives," said Hulda. "The merchants peddling cheap meats, rancid fish, soggy cheese and stale buns. The quality stuff was gone each day before noon. Joseph could find no lodging, his relations were all too distant. Mary looked drawn, weary to the core. I don't think she felt particularly holy or called, Anna, just tired and anxious to get on with it. One look at her and I knew my trip had not been in vain—the child had dropped down ready. My sister protested she could have handled it. 'We take care of our own,' I told her."

"Where did they stay?" asked one woman.

"They were offered a cave behind the inn where some animals were kept, grain stored. Mary and I and one of the maids from the inn scoured the place. The donkey had a separate stall. We bought fresh hay and straw. Joseph borrowed an extra pallet from a cousin. They had their cooking pots from their journey."

"How did the birth go?" Midwives ramble so, offering each detail like a polished gem. I wanted to know the outcome right away. Hulda refused to hurry.

"I had gone back to my sister's to rest and eat after fixing the stable." She paused and slurped her tea. Her eyes glistened. The wrinkles around her mouth twitched. She knew how anxious I was. Her power comes through slow disclosure. I envy her strength of character.

"My sister's husband, smelly big oaf that he is, had just come back from tending his flock. He called for hot soup, strong drink and warmer leggings. He was heading back to the hills for the night. The wolves were hungry in those parts.

The Midwife's Tale

'The night sky is shot through with lights. The high winds whistle strange tunes in the olive branches,' he said in that quiet voice that shepherds have.

"I stared in his cup to see what he was drinking. But his wife just poured his soup and said, 'These are auspicious times!' Whatever that means. She's a bit of a wizard."

Hulda paused and nodded with deference to the prophetess sitting in the corner on the best mat, gumming her bread.

I coughed.

"Oh yes," Hulda sniggered, covering her mouth with her hand. "Well, I had just filled my bowl with fish broth when Joseph burst through the door. 'Her time has come.' He shuddered from the cold wind or the weight of his announcement.

"The shepherd offered a place by the fire, a bowl of soup, a tankard. Joseph thanked him, refused, and sat down to wait for me—jittery as a cat who has a bird to catch. I gulped my soup so fast I burnt my tongue. It stung for a week. I grabbed my bundle and followed him to the stable."

"How was she?" Now that Hulda had reached the climax I could afford to linger with her, savour each moment. No matter how old mothers become, stories of birthing rock their bones.

"She was fine—a happy girl. I washed her in warm water heated by the fire. I arranged the sheets beneath her. I warmed the cloths on a rack by the fire pit. I ordered Joseph out of the place. I told her the tales of birthing. I held her hand when the pains came."

I looked around the room as Hulda's voice gathered strength. The women were swaying forward and backward, remembering their own confinements. Myself, I felt my groin contract, expand with each sentence—letting out the idea of a child, a special child, a grandchild.

103

Mary Woodbury

"Mary cried out, and I mopped her brow with one of the warm cloths that her dear mother Anna sent with her."

I blushed. The women nodded in approval. Hulda went on.

"I lit candles in the corners to ensure safe entrance; I sang the song of the midwives, claiming smooth passage. I prayed the prayer of the bearers. I poured oil on her abdomen, rubbed her back to ease her anguish.

"Mary cried out, 'He's coming. I feel him coming. My little one is struggling to be born. Help me, Hulda.'

"The servant girl arrived to tend the fire. She crooned as she worked. My sister, the midwife of Bethlehem, guarded the door with her ample body, keeping out strangers, encouraging Joseph who paced outside, afraid of our raised voices within."

"Was the birth difficult?" asked the prophetess.

"I know, old woman, I know. Easy birth leads to long life. Hard birth bodes early death. I'm sorry to say, he gave us a hard time. Came out feet first. Push, pant, pause. Push, pant, pause."

Once more I moved my eyes from watching the midwife as she told her tale. The women breathed in unison. Hulda had captured our blood, attuned each body to the passage into life.

Hulda glanced my way. "I was afraid I'd lost him. but your daughter was superb. She put herself in my control. 'Let me be the vessel. You the instrument,' she whispered. She never faltered. We worked together until ..."

"How was he?" I asked, breathless.

"Lusty," she laughed. "I think he started crying in his mother's womb. He came out gasping. Let out a wail that brought his father running. 'It's a boy, then,' he said smiling, standing stupid, gawking. I washed the baby off and gave him to Joseph to hold. A man holding a child is a wonder to behold. They come on magic timidly."

The Midwife's Tale

The women circled in my parlour heaved a pent up sigh. Some straightened skirts, others tugged at lanky hair, Hulda smoothed her apron with her hands.

"And after?" I passed a fresh bowl of dates. "How was Mary?"

"Tired, but pleased. It had taken most of the night. The neighbours dropped by as the sun rose. The shepherds poked their heads in too. My sister and I washed the clothes, swept the floor, made tea."

"Other news?" the old prophetess asked. "Of Bethlehem?"

"One woman died in childbirth. The shepherds linked the lights, the sounds that night with Jesus' birth. My sister put the young folk up while Mary got back her strength."

"When will we see them?" I asked.

"Not for a while," said Hulda. "Joseph decided to try Egypt for a year or two. They need carpenters. Frankly I think the fuss and the folderall of the birth gave him the jitters. He's leery of Herod and his penchant for killing boys with good bloodlines."

The women rose to leave. Each thanked me for the tea and telling. "Mary will be back," I assured them, and myself.

"And is my grandson a good baby?" I asked Hulda as I ushered her through the door. She and the wise woman would walk through town together. I pressed coins into her hand to thank her for the safe delivery.

"He's passing fair, Anna. I just hope his ending is not as painful as his coming."

About the other stories they tell of Jesus' birth, I dare not express opinions. I'm only a woman after all, and was not privy to the telling. I'll say this, though. I held Jesus on my knee when they came home from Egypt. He was a clever lad with dark eyes, like his mother's, that looked into my soul.

105

Mary Woodbury

Crèche

Bert Almon

The nativity pieces,
painted plastic figures,
were unpacked at random
and placed on the tabletop,
forming a strange scene
for a minute or two:
a wise man bowing humbly
to a donkey, the angel
in rapt adoration
staring with cocked head
at the complacent mouth
of a camel. Only Mary seemed right,
looking down tenderly
at a lamb. A few moves made
the cradle cynosure,
and I too looked at it:
the baby with feet joined,
knees raised a little
and arms outstretched
in a crucifixion
without a cross.
My eyes not being plaster,
I had to turn them away.

The First Blended Family

Chris Levan

C hristmas trees are like lightning rods. They catch all the stray family currents, concentrating them in one tremendous jolt of excitement and anxiety. Daily life has its ups and downs, but when you plug in those red and green lights, every peak and valley gets an extra charge.

Oh Help!

Have you noticed how during this season of joy, cutting words come out with a sharper edge? Conversely, hugs are down-to-your-toes warmer. Hands caress more gently and slap with special fierceness. Everything, both tragedy and exultation, seems crisper and clearer.

In a manner similar to birthdays, weddings, funerals and anniversaries, religious high days like Christmas put a fine edge to our memories, reminding us with unsettling clarity of our broken promises and lost hopes. Old recollections seem as yesterday; hurts and hardships regain their forgotten potency.

There are many joys to Christmas, but its chief ache orbits around the problems of being a "happy" family. Looking over the garland-decorated households and our supposedly most intimate relationships, how many of us admit that our family didn't turn out as we expected, as we were led to believe it would?

And what is the family dream? Don't we see it at every department store counter? Whether we have ever experienced it or not, Christmas conjures up the picture of a caring and "complete" family circle gathered 'round a fireplace, the soft glow of contentment flickering off the wall-to-wall smiles.

For many Christians, this image of the perfect family is reinforced each December 25th by the symbolism of the Holy Family. There, at the front of the church or in the market square, they stand in daunting tranquility: Joseph a watchful tower of strength; Mary the perfect mother, always compassionate, understanding; and Jesus, the happy baby who is never a bother—" No crying he makes." There may be a dust storm outside this circle, and the manger may be filled with the refuse of a backwater desert town, but no wrinkle disturbs their silent night, holy night.

The reality is shockingly discordant, isn't it? Many families are pieced together from broken bits—a father is absent due to death or separation. Chilling silences speak loudly of the aunt who refuses to call. The empty mailbox declares that the grandparents are still holding to a decades old grudge. A half-brother grates against his part-time sister. A stepmother struggles to bridge the gap and overcome the wedge that tradition and life circumstance drive between her husband's kids and herself.

And what about the peaceful hearthside chats? Television is the new family altar, and it never lets up on its optimistic jingle bells. Nintendo blinks out a discordant rhythm, and loud music coming from a teenager's room booms out a protest to the Santa sentiments.

Oh yes, there is a pain at the heart of our Christmas families.

Perhaps it is time we set the record straight and saw the First Family of Christmas in another light—as the Bible depicts them.

The First Blended Family

Far from perfect bliss, their experience was similar to our own.

If we take off our "holly jolly" spectacles, we see that the original tale begins with unsettling awkwardness. Mary, the mother of Jesus was pregnant outside of marriage—a precarious position. The law prescribed death by stoning, or an equally punishing return to her father's house. As a fallen, and therefore worthless, daughter, she was utterly vulnerable. Joseph, far from content, is pictured as troubled by the choice he must make—to take Mary home as his wife or risk public scorn. And was it any easier for him to accept the role of step-parent than anyone else? The story reeks of shame and knife-edged disappointment; no wonder they travelled from their home. Let's face it. The Holy Family was a blended family, homeless and destitute, scandal dogging their heels.

So this holiday, be at peace. There is no perfect family. Let the marketing wizards do their worst. Your family, no matter how broken, blended or bent it may be, is blessed—as blessed as that one at the heart of the celebration.

Chris Levan

Biographies

Bert Almon is the author of eight collections of poetry. His seventh book, *Earth Prime*, won the Writers' Guild of Alberta Poetry Award in 1995. Bert lives in Edmonton and teaches creative writing at the University of Alberta.

Timothy J. Anderson's short fiction has appeared in *Prairie Fire* and *Transition*. He has won numerous writing awards, including the Jon Whyte Memorial Essay Prize. His poetry has been set to music by Denis Gougeon, David Parsons, Allen Cole and Clifford Ford, and his first collection, Neurotic Erotica, is slated for fall 1996 release from Slipstream Books. He has also performed opera, musical theatre, and non-musical theatre across Canada, in New York, Singapore, and Hong Kong.

Jacqueline Bell is an Edmonton poet. She has recently completed her first manuscript, *Finding the Pearl*. Her work has been published in *blue buffalo*, *The New Quarterly*, and *Dandelion*. Her work was also included in the anthology *Our Fathers*. She won honourable mention in the Canadian League of Poets national poetry contest in 1994, 1995, and 1996. In 1995, she was co-winner in the *Other Voices* "Sundays" contest.

Cliff Burns has well over 100 published short stories to his credit. They have appeared in eight major anthologies including *The Year's Best Fantasy & Horror* (USA), In Dreams (UK), *Tesseracts III* and *IV* (Canada) and *Das Gross Horror Lesebuch III* and *IV* (Germany). He lives in Regina.

Richard Cumyn's first book of short stories, *The Limit of Delta Y over Delta X*, was published by Goose Lane Editions in 1994. *I Am Not Most Places*, his second book of short stories, was published in September 1996 by Beach Holme Publishing (Vancouver). His stories have also appeared in *The Journey Prize Anthology VI*, *Stag Line: Stories by Men*, and *The Grand-Slam Book of Canadian Baseball Writing*. Richard lives in Kingston.

Jannie Edwards lives and writes in Edmonton. She has been published in several journals and anthoulogies and has been broadcast on CBC radio. She is currently at work on a video project that combines poetry, visual art and American sign language interpretation.

Wynne Edwards wrote training materials during her 25 years as a nurse educator before turning to fiction five years ago. Her work has been published in *Other Voices* and she was a runner-up in their recent "Sundays" contest. She has been honing her editing skills at numerous writing workshops and provided editorial assistance on the *Our Fathers* anthology, published by Rowan Books in 1995.

Betty Gibbs, like many editors, secretly yearns to be a fiction writer. She attended W.O. Mitchell's summer writing workshop in the early 80s, but her novel remains a tantalising prospect rather than a present occupation. Gibbs has been employed full time as an editor for 10 years, after an early career as a teacher and educational media producer. She has attended the Toronto Publishing Workshop on book editing and the Banff Publishing Workshop on educational publishing and currently works for an Edmonton educational publisher, Arnold Publishing.

Barb Howard lives in Bragg Creek, Alberta. Her work has been published in *Freefall* magazine and *blue buffalo*. In 1995, she won the *Canadian Lawyer* short story contest and the 1995 Calgary Writers' Association Sunshine Sketches award. Besides writing she works as a mom and as a legal editor for Carswell legal publications.

Gary J. Langguth lives and writes in Saint John, New Brunswick. His work has been published in Canada, the United States, and England. He also tutors local students, teaches creative writing, serves as contact person for the Saint John Writers' Group and as Second Vice-President of the New Brunswick Writers' Federation.

John B. Lee lives in Brantford, Ontario. He has worked as an editor of several reviews and periodicals and is the author of numerous books of poetry. *These Are the Days of Dogs and Horses*, his most recent poetry collection, was published by Black Moss Press in 1994. Lee won second prize in the CBC Radio literary competition in 1991, and the Milton Acorn Memorial People's Poetry Award in 1993 and 1995.

Chris Levan, principal of St. Stephen's College at the University of Alberta in Edmonton, has published two books with the United Church Publishing House: *The Dancing Steward* and *God Hates Religion*. He writes a weekly column on spirituality and modern society for the *Edmonton Journal* and several other Alberta newspapers. He is a United Church minister.

Dianne Linden, formerly a teacher and a consultant with the Edmonton Public School Board, is currently a graduate student at the University of Alberta. Her writing has appeared in periodicals across Canada and in anthologies in Canada, England, and the United States.

Alice Major is an Edmonton poet and novelist. Her children's book *The Chinese Mirror* won the fourth Alberta Writing for Youth competition. She has also won numerous poetry competitions. Her poetry collection *Time Travels Light*, was published by Rowan Books in 1992. She is past-president of the Writers' Guild of Alberta and an active member of the Stroll of Poets Society.

Marie Anne McLean is a teacher-librarian with Edmonton Public Schools and has been a member of T.A.L.E.S. (The Alberta League Encouraging Storytelling) for 10 years. Her stories appear in the anthologies *Other Prairie Tales: Storytelling for Young Adults* and *What a Story!* an anthology for Junior High students. She is the only Canadian contributor in *Many Voices: True Tales of America Past*.

Biographies

Adele Megann is a Newfoundlander now living in Calgary. She has a background in theological and liturgical studies. Her short fiction has appeared in *Forum, Paperplates, Filling Station, blue buffalo,* and *Secrets from the Orange Couch,* as well as the anthology *Boundless Alberta.* In 1995, she won the second annual Bronwen Wallace Memorial Award. She is currently Fiction Co-editor of *Dandelion* magazine.

Syr Ruus was born in Estonia, educated in the United States, and has lived in rural Nova Scotia for many years teaching elementary school. A beginning writer, Syr recently won first prize in the Nova Scotia Writers' Federation Writing for Children competition.

Shirley A. Serviss is an Edmonton writer, creative writing instructor and theology student. She has published poetry and essays in numerous literary magazines and anthologies. Her first poetry collection, *Model Families,* was short listed for the 1992 Book of the Year by the Book Publishers Association of Alberta.

Sybil Shaw-Hamm writes back in the bush of Steinbach, Manitoba, between freedom and isolation, between taking her writing seriously and not. Her poetry and short stories have appeared in *Broomstick, Other Voices,* and *Zygote.* She won the "Sundays" Short Story Contest in *Other Voices* in 1995 and the Canadian Authors Association (Manitoba Branch) Fiction Contest in 1996.

Biographies

Gail Sidonie Sobat's poetry and fiction have appeared in a number of journals including *Whetstone, The Prairie Journal of Canadian Literature, Other Voices* and *JCT: An Interdisciplinary Journal of Canadian Studies.* Her work has been broadcast on CBC's Alberta Anthology and performed at the Edmonton Fringe. Her first academic article was recently published in *Children's Literature Association Quarterly* (Winter 1996).

Anne Swannell was born in London, England, went to high school in Calgary, Alberta, lived in Edmonton from 1966–1968 and is currently the art instructor for the South Island Distance Education School on Vancouver Island. Her most recent poetry collection, *Mall*, was published by Rowan Books in 1993.

Mary Woodbury lives in Edmonton and has been active in the Alberta writing community for many years. Her children's books include *A Gift for Johnny Know It All, Where in the World is Jenny Parker?, Letting Go,* and *The Invisible Polly McDoodle.* Her upcoming novel, *The Runaway Grandpa,* short listed for the Alberta Writing for Youth Competition, will be published by Coteau Books in 1997. *Fruitbodies,* a collection of her poetry for grown-ups, was released in 1996 by River Books.